"I can't stay here now. I'll have to go back."

"No!"

The word was torn from him. She couldn't be serious. To go back to a man who clearly had no respect—let alone any love—for her…

He wanted her, he realized, even as he rejected the thought as unworthy of him. This was no fantasy; this was real, this was honest—though he doubted she'd believe his feelings had no strings attached. She'd probably find any overture he made toward her—however innocent—utterly repulsive. He wasn't arrogant enough to believe she felt any attraction to him. Yet still he prolonged the moment. And, as if becoming aware that the atmosphere between them had changed, she struggled to get up.

"Please," she said, and although there was no fear in her eyes, there was withdrawal. And a mute appeal he found hard to resist.

"You do please…me," he told her huskily. And he was sure that, despite herself, she gave a helpless little moan.

New York Times bestselling author **ANNE MATHER** has written since she was seven, but it was only when her first child was born that she fulfilled her dream of becoming a writer. Her first book, *Caroline,* appeared in 1966. It was immediately successful, and since then Anne has written more than 140 novels, reaching a readership that spans the world.

Born and raised in the north of England, Anne still makes her home there with her husband, two children and, now, grandchildren. Asked if she finds writing a lonely occupation, she replies that her characters always keep her company. In fact, she is so busy sorting out their lives that she often doesn't have time for her own! An avid reader herself, she devours everything from sagas and romances to mainstream fiction and suspense. Anne has also written a number of mainstream novels, with *Dangerous Temptation* her most recent title, published by MIRA® Books.

Books by Anne Mather

HARLEQUIN PRESENTS®
2248—THE SPANIARD'S SEDUCTION

Anne Mather

HOT PURSUIT

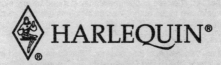

HARLEQUIN®

TORONTO • NEW YORK • LONDON
AMSTERDAM • PARIS • SYDNEY • HAMBURG
STOCKHOLM • ATHENS • TOKYO • MILAN • MADRID
PRAGUE • WARSAW • BUDAPEST • AUCKLAND

ISBN 0-373-12285-3

HOT PURSUIT

First North American Publication 2002.

Copyright © 2002 by Anne Mather.

This edition published by arrangement with Harlequin Books S.A.

® and TM are trademarks of the publisher. Trademarks indicated with
® are registered in the United States Patent and Trademark Office, the
Canadian Trade Marks Office and in other countries.

Visit us at www.eHarlequin.com

Printed in U.S.A.

CHAPTER ONE

'WE'RE going to be late, Daddy.'

'I know that.'

Matt Seton managed not to sound as frustrated as he felt. It wasn't Rosie's fault that he'd overslept on the very morning that Mrs Webb wasn't here, or that his head was still buzzing with the effort of falling out of bed just a couple of hours after he'd flaked out.

'Mrs Sanders says that there's no excuse for sleeping in these days,' continued Rosie primly, and Matt could hear the echo of his ex-wife Carol's peevish tones in his daughter's voice.

'I know. I know. I'm sorry.' Clenching his teeth, Matt tightened his hands on the wheel of the powerful Range Rover. The temptation was to step down hard on the accelerator, but he didn't think that risking another ticket for speeding would improve his standing with Mrs Sanders either.

'So who's going to pick me up this afternoon?' Rosie asked, a little anxiously now, and Matt turned to give his daughter a reassuring look.

'I will,' he told the seven-year-old firmly. 'And if I can't make it I'll ask Auntie Emma to collect you. How's that?'

Rosie seemed slightly mollified, but as her small hands curved around the bag containing her pencil case and schoolbooks she cast her father an appealing look. 'You won't forget, will you, Daddy? I don't like having to ask Mrs Sanders to ring you.'

Matt expelled a long sigh. 'You've only had to do that once, Rosie,' he protested. And then, because it was obviously a cause of some concern to the child, his lean mouth parted in a rueful grin. 'I'll be there,' he promised. 'I can't have my best girl waiting around in the playground.'

'Mrs Sanders doesn't let us wait in the playground,' Rosie

told him pedantically. 'We have to stay in school if our Mummys or Daddys aren't there when school's over.'

'Right.' Matt's mouth compressed. 'Well, as I say, I won't let you down. Okay?'

'Okay!'

Rosie's eyes brightened in anticipation and Matt felt a heel for even comparing her to her mother. Rosemary was nothing like Carol, thank God, and it was up to him to organise a more stable structure in his daughter's life.

And he was trying, goodness knew. Since ill-health had forced Rosie's original nanny to retire he had interviewed a number of applicants for the position without any lasting success. Few younger women wanted to live in a remote area of Northumbria, far from the nearest town, and the older nannies who'd applied had, for the most part, appeared far too strict for his taste. He didn't want Rosie's confidence, already fragile because of her mother's abandonment, shattered by some fire-breathing dragon who saw the unconventionality of Matt's life-style as an opportunity to terrorise the little girl.

In consequence, he was seriously considering contacting an agency in London, in the hope that someone there might be professional enough about their career not to care about living in such rural surroundings. Saviour's Bay wasn't the back of beyond, after all. It was a wild and beautiful area of the Northumbrian coast, whose history was as turbulent as the seas that lashed the rocks below the cliffs. Its moors and hamlets were the haunt of archaeologists and naturalists, and from Matt's point of view it was the ideal place to escape the demands that being a successful writer had put on him. Few people knew where he lived these days, and that suited him very well.

But it didn't suit everyone, he acknowledged, and until the day came when he was forced to consider sending Rosie away to school he had to persist in his search for a suitable replacement for the woman who had virtually brought her up.

Not her mother, needless to say, he added to himself. Carol's indifference, not just to him but also to their daughter, had long since lost its power to hurt him. There were times when he wondered why they'd ever married at all, but Carol had given him Rosie, and he could never regret that. He adored his small daughter and he'd do whatever it took to keep her with him.

Matt appreciated that his success had given him certain advantages. When Carol had left him for another man he'd been the author of two moderately successful novels, but that was all. It was his third book that had hit the big time, and his fourth and fifth novels had sold in their millions. Subsequent sales of screen rights to a hotshot Hollywood director had helped, and these days he could virtually name his price.

But being photographed wherever he went, having his picture exhibited in magazines and periodicals, being invited onto television talk shows and the like, was not what he'd had in mind when he'd written his first book. As a doctor, specialising in psychology, he knew exactly what other people thought he'd expected from his change of career. The truth was, he had never been interested in becoming famous. And these days he just wanted to be left alone to get on with his next manuscript.

Which was why he'd bought Seadrift, the sprawling house overlooking the bay that he'd fallen in love with the first time he'd seen it. It served the dual purpose of giving him the peace he needed to work and the opportunity to put several hundred miles between him and the London media.

The gates of St Winifred's Primary loomed ahead and Matt breathed a sigh of relief. A glance at his watch told him it was still a minute or two to nine o'clock, and if Rosie got her skates on she should make it into class in time for registration.

'Have a good day, angel,' he said, exchanging a swift kiss with his daughter before she thrust open her door and clambered down onto the kerb.

'Bye, Daddy,' she called, her face briefly exhibiting a little of the anxiety she'd exhibited earlier. Then, cramming her grey hat with its upturned brim and distinctive red band down onto her sooty bob, to prevent the wind from taking it, she raised a hand in farewell and raced across the playground to the doors, where one or two stragglers were still entering the building.

Matt waited until the swirling hem of Rosie's pleated skirt had disappeared from view before putting the Range Rover into

drive again and moving away. He couldn't prevent the sigh of
relief he felt at knowing that she was in safe hands for a few
hours at least. When he was working he could easily forget the
time, and it wasn't fair on his daughter that she should have to
spend her days worrying that he might not be there when she
came out of school.

That was why he needed someone—nursemaid, nanny, whatever—to take up the slack. He had a housekeeper, Mrs Webb,
who came in most days to cook and clean and do the ironing,
but he'd never realised how much he'd depended on Hester
Gibson until she'd been forced to retire. But then, Hester had
been so much more than a nanny. From the very beginning
she'd been more of a mother to Rosie than Carol had ever been,
and when Carol had moved in with her lover Hester had taken
Matt under her wing, too.

They had been living in London at that time, but Hester had
had no qualms when Matt had suggested moving to the wilds
of Northumbria. Like Matt, she had been an exile from the
northeast of England herself, only living in the south because
she hadn't been able to find suitable employment in her home
town of Newcastle. It had been like coming home for both of
them, and the house at Saviour's Bay had offered space and
comfort.

Matt sighed again, and, turning the heavy vehicle in the yard
of the village pub, drove back the way he'd come. The roads
between Saviour's Bay and the village of Ellsmoor, where
Rosie's school was situated, were narrow, with high, untrimmed
hedges on either side. He supposed the state of the hedges was
due to the local farmers, who were having a hard time of it at
present, but it meant it was impossible to see far enough ahead
to overtake the slow-moving hay wagon in front of him. But
Matt was in no hurry now. He had the rest of the morning and
the early part of the afternoon to himself, and as he'd worked
half the night he thought he deserved a break.

Of course, he needed a shave, he conceded, running a hand
over the stubble on his jawline. And some coffee, he thought
eagerly, having only had time to pour milk onto Rosie's cornflakes and fill her glass with fresh orange juice before charging

out to the car. Yes, some strong caffeine was just what he needed. It might clear his head and provide him with the impetus to get this nanny business sorted.

He made reasonably good time back to the house. Saviour's Bay was a village, too, but a much smaller community than that of Ellsmoor. In recent weeks he'd toyed with the idea of buying an apartment in Newcastle that they could use in term time. A would-be employee would obviously find the city more appealing. But the idea of living in town—any town—even for a limited period wasn't appealing to him. He loved Seadrift, loved its isolation too much to consider any alternative at present. And Rosie loved it, too. She couldn't remember living anywhere else.

As he swung onto the private road that led up to the house he noticed a car parked at an angle at the side of the road just before the turning. He slowed, wondering if the driver had missed his way, but the vehicle appeared to be deserted. Whoever owned the car had either abandoned it to walk back to the village, or had gone up to the house, he decided. There were no other houses along this stretch of the cliffs, which was why he'd bought Seadrift in the first place.

He frowned, looking back the way he'd come, but there was no one in sight. He wasn't worried. He'd had too many skirmishes with the press in the past to be concerned about some rogue reporter who might have hopes of finding a novel perspective on his present situation. Thankfully the press in this area accepted his presence without much hassle, and were usually too busy following up local issues to trouble him. But the car was there and it had to belong to someone.

So who?

Scowling, he pressed his foot down on the accelerator and quickened his pace. The pleasant anticipation he'd been feeling of making coffee and reading his mail was dissipating, and he resented whoever it was for ruining his mood.

The gates to the house appeared on the right. They were open, as usual, and Matt drove straight through and up the white gravelled drive to the house. Long and low and sprawling, Seadrift looked solidly inviting, even on this overcast June morning. Its walls were shadowed with wisteria, its tall windows reflecting the light of the watery sun that was trying to push between the clouds.

There was a block-paved turning circle in front of the double doors, flanked by outbuildings that had now been put to a variety of uses. A triple garage had been converted from a low barn, and another of the sheds was used to store gardening equipment.

Parking the Range Rover to one side of the doors, Matt sat for a moment, waiting to see if his arrival elicited any response from whoever it was he suspected had invaded his territory. And, sure enough, a figure did appear from around the corner of the barn. But it wasn't the man he'd expected; it was a woman. And as far as he could see she was carrying nothing more incriminating than the handbag-size haversack that was looped over one shoulder.

She was young, too, he noticed, watching her as she saw the car and after only a momentary hesitation came towards him. She was reasonably tall and slim, with long light brown hair streaked with blonde and confined in a chunky braid. She didn't look any older than her mid-twenties, and he wondered what she was doing, wandering around a stranger's property. Hadn't she heard of the dangers that could face young women like her in remote areas? Hell, in not so remote ones, too. For God's sake, she knew nothing about him.

Of course, she might have expected there to be a woman at the house, he was reminding himself, when another thought struck him. She could be from the agency. Just because he hadn't heard from them recently it didn't mean they didn't still have his name on their books. Here he was, suspecting the worst, and she could be the best thing that had happened to him in weeks. A nanny for Rosie. Someone to look after her and care for her; to give her her meals and be company for her when he was working. Someone to take her to school and pick her up again on those occasions when he couldn't. Could he be that lucky?

Collecting his thoughts, Matt pushed open the door of the Range Rover and stepped out onto the forecourt. Then, replacing his scowl with a polite look of enquiry, he went towards her and said, 'Are you looking for me?'

'Oh—' The girl seemed taken aback by his sudden appearance and Matt had a moment to assess the quality of the cream leather jacket she had slung about her shoulders. It had obviously not been bought off the peg at some department store, and the voile dress she was wearing with it seemed unsuitable for a morning interview with a prospective employer. But what the hell? he thought. Professionally trained nannies could command generous salaries these days, and what did he know about women's fashions anyway?

Apparently deciding he meant her no harm, in spite of the stubble on his chin, she gave a nervous smile. 'I—yes,' she said, answering his question. 'Yes, I suppose I am. If—if you live here.'

'I do.' Matt held out his hand. 'Matt Seton. And you are...?'

She seemed disconcerted by his introduction. Had she recognised his name? Whatever, she was definitely reluctant to shake his hand. But eventually she allowed him to enclose her fingers in his much larger ones and said, 'I'm—Sara.' And, when he arched his brow, 'Um—Sara Victor.'

'Ah.' Matt liked her name. It sounded solid; old-fashioned. Having interviewed a series of Hollys and Jades and Pippas, it was refreshing to meet someone whose parents hadn't been influenced by television soaps. 'So, Miss Victor: have you come far?'

She seemed surprised at his question, withdrawing her hand from his with unflattering haste. Dammit, surely she wasn't scared of him.

'Er—not far,' she said at last. Then, when it was obvious that something more was expected, she added, 'I—I stayed at a guesthouse in Morpeth last night.'

'Really?' Matt revised his opinion. The agency must have cast its net far and wide. She'd hardly have stayed in Morpeth if she lived in Newcastle. There was only a handful of miles between the two.

'Is that your car at the end of the road?' he asked now, and she nodded.

'It's a hired car,' she told him swiftly. 'But there seems to be something wrong with it. It gave up down there, as you can see.'

'Lucky you made it this far, then,' remarked Matt neutrally. 'I'll have the garage in Saviour's Bay pick it up later. They can return it to the agency when it's fixed.'

'But I don't—' She broke off, staring at him as if he was speaking in a foreign language. 'There's no need for you to do that. If I could just use your phone—'

Her voice trailed away and Matt's brows drew together in sudden suspicion. 'You're not from the agency, are you?' he exclaimed. 'I should have known. You're another bloody reporter, aren't you?' He gave her a scathing look. 'They must be desperate if they're sending bimbos to do the job!'

'I am not a bimbo!' For once he had stung her into an unconsidered retort. She straightened her spine, as if she could add to her height. But she was still several inches shorter than Matt's six feet plus and her frustration showed in her face. 'And I never claimed to be from any agency.'

'Whatever.' Matt's jaw compressed. 'So, what are you doing here? I notice you haven't denied being a reporter.'

'A reporter?' She stared at him, thick blonde lashes shading eyes of a misty grey-green. 'I don't understand. Were you expecting a reporter?' Her face paled a little. 'Why would a reporter come here?'

'Don't pretend you don't know who I am.'

'I don't.' She frowned. 'Well, I know your name is Seton. You told me that.'

'Matt Seton?' prompted Matt caustically. 'Ring any bells?'

'Actually, no.' She looked troubled. 'Who are you?'

Matt swayed back on his heels. Was she serious? She certainly looked as if she was, and if he'd had any conceit to speak of she'd have certainly exploded it with her innocent words. If they were innocent, he amended. Or could she really be that good?

'You don't go to bookshops, then?' he enquired drily, aware of a totally unfamiliar sensation of pique. 'You've never heard of my work?'

'I'm afraid not.' She looked a little relieved now, but hardly apologetic. 'Are you famous?'

Matt couldn't prevent an ironic laugh. 'Moderately so,' he said mildly. 'So...' He lifted his shoulders. 'What are you doing here?'

'I told you. My car broke down.' She paused. 'I was hoping to use your phone, as I said.'

'Really?' Matt considered her.

'Yes, really.' She shivered suddenly, and, although it was hardly a cold morning, Matt noticed how pale she was. 'Um, would you mind?'

Matt hesitated. It could still be a clever ruse on her part to get inside his house. But he was beginning to doubt that. Nevertheless, no one apart from his friends and family had ever got beyond his door, and he was loath to invite any stranger, however convincing, into his home.

'Don't you have a mobile?' he said, and she gave a weary sigh.

'I don't have my mobile with me,' she told him tiredly. 'But if helping me is a problem just tell me where I can find the nearest garage. I assume the one you mentioned isn't far away.'

'Far enough,' muttered Matt heavily. 'Can you walk the best part of three miles?'

'If I have to,' she replied, lifting her head. 'Just point me in the right direction.'

But he couldn't do it. Berating himself for being a fool, he slammed the door of the Range Rover and gestured towards the house. 'You can use the phone,' he said, striding past her. He led the way through an archway that gave access to the back of the building, hoping he wasn't making the biggest mistake of his life. 'Follow me.'

Immediately, his two retrievers set up an excited barking, and he wondered if she'd heard them earlier. Although the dogs themselves were just big pussy-cats, really, the noise they made had scared off tougher intruders than her.

'Do you like dogs?' he asked, glancing over his shoulder, and she gave an uncertain shrug.

'I don't know,' she said. 'Are yours dangerous?'

'Oh, yeah!' Matt gave a wry grin. Then, realising she was taking him literally, he added. 'Dangerously friendly, I mean. If you're not careful they'll lick you to death.'

Her smile appeared again, a more open one this time, and Matt was amazed at the difference it made to her thin features. For a moment she looked really beautiful, but then the smile disappeared again and he was left with the knowledge that for someone who had supposedly only been driving for about an hour that morning she looked exhausted.

Opening the door into the boot room, Matt weathered the assault of the two golden retrievers with good-natured indulgence. They were Rosie's dogs, really, but as they spent as much time with him as they did with her they tended to share their affections equally.

It took them only a few moments to discover he wasn't alone, however, and he had to grab them by the scruffs of their necks before they knocked his guest over. As it was, she swayed a little under the onslaught, and he was forced to lock the dogs in their compound in the yard before opening the door into the kitchen.

'Sorry about that,' he said, glancing ruefully about him. Their plates from the previous night's supper still lay on the drainer, waiting to be put into the dishwasher, and Rosie's breakfast bowl and glass occupied a prominent position on the island bar. If Mrs Webb had been working that morning the place would have looked much different, and Matt thought how typical it was that the one morning he had a visitor the kitchen should look like a tip.

'They're very friendly, aren't they?' she said, speaking about the dogs, but he knew she'd noticed the mess. 'Are they yours or your wife's?'

Matt's mouth turned down. 'My daughter's, actually,' he said. Then, because she was looking as if the next puff of wind would knock her over, he added, 'I was just about to make myself some coffee. Would you like a cup?'

'Oh, please!'

If he was to speculate, Matt would have said she spoke like someone who hadn't had anything to eat or drink in some time.

There was such eagerness in her response, and once again he felt a renewal of his doubts about her. Who was she really? Where had she been heading on the coast road, which was usually only used by locals and holidaymakers? What did she really want?

'I've got the number of the garage in Saviour's Bay,' he said as he spooned coffee into the filter. 'I'll just get this going and then I'll find it for you.'

'Thank you.'

She hovered by the door, one hand clutching the strap of her haversack, the other braced against the wall unit nearest to her. He couldn't be sure, but he thought she was trembling, though whether that was because she was cold, despite the warmth of the Aga, or apprehensive, he wouldn't like to say.

It was quite a novelty for Matt to face the fact that she might not trust him. Her question about whether the dogs belonged to him or his wife might just have been a rather clumsy attempt to discover if he was married. For the first time he realised how vulnerable she might feel.

'Hey, why don't you sit down?' he suggested, pointing towards the two stools that were set at either side of the island bar. 'This is going to take a few minutes.'

'O—kay.'

With evident reluctance she crossed the room and, dropping her haversack onto the floor beside her, levered herself onto one of the tall stools. But he noticed she chose the one that put the width of the bar between them, before treating him to another of those polite smiles.

Matt pulled a wry face but he didn't say anything. She'd learn soon enough that he wasn't interested in her or anyone else. That was, if she bothered to check him out in whatever place she was heading for. Despite his fame, and the monetary success it had brought him, Matt had declined all opportunities to replace his ex-wife.

And he had had opportunities, he conceded without conceit. A man in his position always attracted a certain type of woman, even if he was as ugly as sin, and he wasn't that. His features were harsh, maybe, but they weren't totally unappealing. He'd been told when he was younger and less cynical that deep-set eyes, olive skin, and a nose that had been broken playing rugby were far more interesting than pretty-boy looks.

But who knew what the real truth was? He no longer cared. So long as Rosie loved him, that was all that mattered.

When he turned back to his visitor, however, he got a surprise. While he'd been speculating on the possibilities of her being afraid of him, she'd slumped in her seat, shoulders hunched, head resting on the arms she'd folded on the counter. She was either asleep or exhausted, he realised in amazement. And he'd bet money on the former. What the hell was going on?

The phone rang at that moment and at once she jerked awake. Cursing, Matt went to answer it, not knowing whether his irritation was caused by the fact that she'd fallen asleep or that the sound had awakened her. Looping the receiver off the wall, he jammed it to his ear. 'Yeah?'

'Matt?'

'Emma!' Matt expelled a long breath. 'Hi! What can I do for you?'

'I'm not disturbing you, am I?'

It would be all the same if she was, thought Matt ruefully. He owed Emma Proctor too much to resent the interruption and, aware that Sara was watching him with wary grey-green eyes, he said swiftly, 'No, I just got back from taking Rosie to school. I'm in the middle of making some coffee, actually. I'm afraid we slept in this morning.'

Emma made a sympathetic sound. 'Of course, it's Mrs Webb's day off, isn't it? I gather you've had no luck with the agency?'

'No.' Matt didn't particularly want to get into that now. 'No luck at all.'

'What about trying the local employment agency?' Emma suggested helpfully. 'They sometimes have childminders on their books.'

'But I don't want a childminder,' declared Matt mildly. 'I want someone with the proper training, not a girl who only wants to work here on a part-time basis. I need someone in the evenings, too, when I'm working. You know that.'

'What you need is a surrogate mother for Rosie,' said Emma a little tersely. 'And the chances of finding someone like that who's also prepared to live in rural Northumbria—'

'I know, I know.' He and Emma had had this conversation too many times for Matt to show much patience with it now. 'Look, thanks for caring, but I've really got to work this out for myself.'

'If you can,' muttered Emma huffily. 'Anyway, that wasn't why I rang. I wondered if you wanted me to collect Rosie from school this afternoon. I've got to go to Berwick this morning, but I should be back by—'

'It's okay. I've told Rosie I'll pick her up myself this afternoon,' replied Matt quickly, wondering what his visitor was making of the one-sided conversation. He hesitated. 'I appreciate the offer, Em. I really do. Some other time, yeah?'

'I suppose so.' To his relief, she didn't pursue it. 'Well, I'd better go. There's nothing you want from Berwick, is there? I can always drop it off on my way home.'

'Not that I can think of,' said Matt politely. 'Have a good day, Em. Speak to you soon.'

When he replaced the receiver he noticed that his visitor dropped her gaze, as if afraid of being caught out watching him. Frowning slightly, he turned back to the filter and saw that the jug was now full and steaming on the hotplate. Unhooking a couple of mugs from the rack, he looked at Sara again.

'Black? White? With sugar or without?'

'White with no sugar,' she answered at once. 'It smells delicious.'

Matt poured some for her and pushed the mug across the counter. Then, taking a carton of milk from the fridge, he passed that over, too. 'Help yourself.'

'Thank you.'

Matt drew a breath. 'You hungry?'

'Hungry?' For a moment she looked almost eager. Then those thick blonde lashes shaded her eyes again. 'No,' she responded carefully. 'This is fine.'

Matt considered, and then pulled a large biscuit tin towards him. It was where Mrs Webb stored the muffins she made for his breakfast and, although these had been made the day before, they still smelled fresh and appetising. Heated in the microwave, they often made a meal for someone who often forgot about food altogether, and Matt offered the tin to Sara now.

'Sure?' he asked. 'I usually heat a couple of these for my breakfast. I can recommend them.'

She looked as if she wanted to take one, but after a pregnant pause she shook her head. 'The coffee is all I need,' she assured him. And then, perhaps to divert herself, she added, 'I gather you're looking for a nursemaid for your daughter?' Faint colour entered her cheeks. 'How old is she?'

'Rosie?'

Matt hesitated, closing the tin again. Then, deciding there was no harm in telling her, he added, 'Seven.' He shook his head. 'I can hardly believe it. Time goes so fast.'

Sara moistened her lips. 'Is your wife dead?' she asked, and then lifted her hand in a gesture of remorse. 'No. Don't answer that. I had no right to ask.'

'No, you didn't.' But Matt answered her just the same. 'Carol left me when Rosie was a baby,' he said flatly. 'Don't worry. It's not a secret.'

'I see.' Sara cradled her coffee mug between her palms. 'I'm sorry.'

'Yeah.' Matt gave a wry smile. 'But, believe me, it was the best thing for both of us.'

Sara looked up at him. 'For you and your wife?'

'For me and my daughter,' Matt amended, hooking his heel around the stool opposite and straddling it to face her. He nodded to her cup. 'Coffee all right?'

She drew back when he was seated, as if his nearness—or his bulk—intimidated her. It crossed his mind that someone must have done a number on her, must be responsible for her lack of confidence, but he didn't say anything. In his professional experience it was wiser not to probe another person's psyche. Not unless you had a reason for doing so, at least.

'So you live here alone?' she said at last, apparently deciding to pursue her enquiries, and he pulled a wry face.

'I have Rosie,' he said, his lips twitching. 'Hey, are you sure you're not a journalist? That's the kind of question they ask.'

Her face fell. 'No!' she exclaimed. And then, as if realising he was only teasing her, she continued, 'I was thinking about the job.'

'What job?' For a moment he was nonplussed, and she took advantage of his silence.

'Your daughter's nanny,' she declared quickly. 'Would you consider me for the post?'

CHAPTER TWO

HE LOOKED stunned. That was the only description Sara could find to fit the expression on his lean tanned face. An expression that was definitely at odds with his harsh compelling features. At least a day's growth of stubble roughened his jawline and there were dark pouches beneath the deep-set hollows of his eyes.

And why shouldn't he be shocked at her announcement? thought Sara uneasily. It wasn't every day that a strange woman turned up on your doorstep asking for work. After all, he knew nothing about her. She didn't even have the backing of an employment agency. She could be a con artist, living on her wits. Though any con artist worth her salt would surely not try and dupe a man like him.

Sara wished now that she hadn't made the offer. She didn't know anything about him either, and just because he had been kind to her that was no reason to trust him. Besides, she wasn't a nanny. She wasn't a nursemaid. Her experience with children had been confined to the classroom, but he'd never believe that she'd once been a primary school teacher. That had been at another time; sometimes now it seemed like another life. When she'd been young—and so naïve.

'You're offering to become Rosie's nanny?' Matt Seton asked at last, and she could tell he was suspicious of her offer. 'You didn't say you were looking for work.'

I'm not. I'm looking for sanctuary, thought Sara wildly, but she couldn't tell him that. And when she'd left London the previous evening she'd had no plans beyond the need to get away. To put as many miles between her and Max as possible.

But she couldn't think about that now. She needed time to come to terms with what she'd done. 'I might be,' she said, taking a sip of her coffee to avoid his penetrating gaze. 'Are you interested?'

' "I might be", ' he mocked, echoing her words. 'Are you used to working with children.'

'I was.' Sara chose her words with care. She didn't like lying but she really didn't have a choice. And, the more she thought about it, the more the idea appealed to her. A job like this might be exactly what she needed. Somewhere to stay; a means of earning money; a chance to disappear without leaving a trail. She hesitated, and then stated bravely, 'I used to be a primary school teacher.'

'Used to be?' Dark brows arched interrogatively.

'Yes.'

'But not any more?'

'Not recently, no.'

'Why?' The question was innocent enough but she had the feeling he was baiting her.

'Because I gave up teaching some time ago,' she admitted. 'But it's not something you forget.'

'So what have you been doing?'

Fighting for my life!

Somehow she managed to keep her voice steady as she replied, 'I—got married. My hus—my ex-husband, that is, didn't like me having a job.'

And that must be the understatement of the year!

'I see.' Matt Seton was regarding her so intently she was almost sure he could see into her mind. And if he could he'd know that she wasn't being completely honest, that she was only telling him as much of the truth as she needed to sound sincere. 'Do you come from around here?'

He asked a lot of questions. Sara swallowed and considered the option of saying yes. But he'd know she didn't sound like a local. So, after a moment, she said, 'I used to live in the south of England until quite recently.'

'Until you decided to hire a car and drive three hundred miles up the motorway?' suggested Matt laconically. 'What happened, Sara? Did your husband ditch you for someone else, so you decided to disappear and make the bastard sweat?'

'No!' She was horrified. If Max had turned his attentions elsewhere she wouldn't be in this state now. 'I—I told you, we're—

we're divorced. I just fancied a change of scene, that's all. I didn't know where I wanted to stay until I got here.'

'And decided that because I needed a nanny, you'd be it,' he commented cynically. 'Forgive me if I sound sceptical, but I've never heard such a load of garbage in my life.'

'It's not garbage.' Sara suspected she was beginning to sound desperate but she couldn't help it. She really wanted this job. 'Do you want a nanny or don't you? You sounded fairly sure about it when you were on the phone.'

Matt tipped his stool onto its back legs, balancing himself with one hand on the counter. 'So you were listening?'

'How could I not?' Sara knew there was no point in denying it. 'All I'm asking is that you consider me for the position.'

'Really?' He didn't look convinced. 'So what qualifications do you have?'

Sara hesitated. 'Well, two years of working at a primary school in—in London.' She'd almost mentioned the school's name and that would have been foolish. 'Like I say, I left when I got married.'

'And you can prove this? You've got certification, references?'

Sara bent her head. 'Not with me.'

'But you could get them?'

Her shoulders slumped. 'Not easily, no.'

'Surprise, surprise.' He was sardonic. 'Hey, I may live in the sticks, but I haven't got straw in my ears, Mrs Victor.'

'It's Miss Victor,' she muttered unnecessarily. If he wasn't going to employ her, what did it matter what he thought her name was? It wasn't her real one. She lifted her head, deciding to make one last plea for his understanding. 'Look, I'm not going to pretend that working for you wouldn't suit my purposes. It would. And, although I can't prove it, I was a primary school teacher. A damn good one, as it happens.' She gazed at him. 'You could give me a week's trial, at least. What have you got to lose?'

'Plenty.' The feet of the stool thudded down onto the tiled floor as he leaned almost threateningly towards her. 'I don't just leave my daughter with anyone, *Miss* Victor. She's far too important to me. I'm sorry.'

He didn't look sorry. On the contrary, he looked as if he'd be glad to see the back of her, and she pushed the remains of her coffee aside and got to her feet.

'So am I,' she said, barely audibly, bending to pick up her bag. 'If—if I could just use your phone...'

'Wait.' To her dismay he stood also, successfully putting himself between her and the door. 'Tell me something: did you really spend the night in Morpeth, or was that a lie, too?'

'Does it matter?'

She was trying to remain calm, but she was suddenly conscious of how vulnerable she was here. So long as they'd been discussing the job she'd felt a certain amount of control over the situation. But he'd made it plain that he didn't believe her and now she was uneasily aware that he held her fate in his hands. What did he intend to do with that knowledge? What if he decided to report her to the authorities? How long would she remain free if he gave her description to the police?

'Humour me,' he said, pushing his hands into the back pockets of his jeans. Jeans that fit him so closely that they were worn almost white in places, she noticed inconsequentially, running her tongue over her dry lips.

'I—all right, no,' she conceded unwillingly. 'May I use the phone now?'

'So—you've been driving since late last night or early this morning?'

Sara sighed. 'Something like that.'

'You must be exhausted.'

She gave a mirthless laugh. 'What's it to you?'

He was silent for so long that she thought he wasn't going to answer her. Then he said flatly, 'I'm not completely heartless. I know a runaway when I see one. Why don't you sit down again and I'll make you some breakfast? You might even like to rest for a while before contacting the garage about your car.'

Sara stared at him. 'I didn't come down with the last shower either,' she exclaimed scornfully. 'And where do you get off, calling me a runaway? I told you, I decided I needed a change of scene—'

'I know what you said,' he interrupted her blandly. 'But you don't really expect me to believe that, do you?'

'I don't give a—a flying flea what you believe!'

'Oh, I think you do.' He was smug.

'Why should I?'

'Because it must have occurred to you that I could decide to keep you here until I had your story checked out.'

Sara gasped. 'You wouldn't do that!'

'Give me one reason why I shouldn't.'

'Because—because you have no right. I'm not a child; I'm not even a teenager. I can please myself what I do.'

'Possibly.' He paused. 'But you must admit that someone who suddenly decides they need a change of scene wouldn't leave in the middle of the night. Particularly as you appear to have left without bringing any papers, any references, anything to prove you are who you say you are.'

Sara felt totally defeated. 'Just let me go,' she said wearily. 'Please.' She paused. 'Forget the phone. I'll check the car myself, and if it still doesn't start I'll make some other arrangement. Just forget you ever saw me.'

Matt sighed. 'I can't do that.'

'Why not?'

'Because I think you need some help,' he said gently. 'Why don't you tell me what really happened? My guess is that you had a row with your husband and decided to take off. I don't know where the hired car comes in, but that's not important. Am I somewhere near the truth?'

'I told you.' She spoke doggedly. 'I don't have a husband.'

'Right.' His mouth thinned. 'So why are you still wearing both your wedding and engagement rings? For sentimental reasons?'

Sara sagged. She'd forgotten about the rings. She was so used to wearing them, so used to Max's anger if she ever dared to take them off, that she hadn't even thought about them or what they might mean to someone else.

She swayed. She felt so dizzy suddenly. When had she last had anything to eat? she wondered. Not today, certainly. And she couldn't recall eating much the previous day either. She'd missed dinner, of course, but had she had any lunch? She wished she could remember. But everything that had happened before Max came home remained a blank.

Not the memory of Max lying at the foot of the stairs, however. She recalled that, and recalled herself rushing down the stairs after him, kneeling at his side, desperately trying to find a pulse. But her hand had been shaking so much she hadn't been able to feel anything. In any case, he hadn't been breathing. And surely that could mean only one thing.

He was dead!

She swayed again, and saw Matt put out his hand towards her. He was going to touch her, she thought, jerking back from the contact as if she was stung. Her legs felt like jelly. Dear God, what was happening to her? She mustn't pass out here. She knew nothing about this man except that he was threatening to expose her.

She should never have come here; never have asked for his help. She was on her own now. That was what she wanted. The only person she could rely on was herself...

Sara opened her eyes to curtains moving in the breeze from the open window behind them. Sunlight dappled peach-coloured walls, laid yellow fingers over a tall armoire and a matching chest of drawers, added warmth to the lime-green quilted bedspread that covered her. Somewhere a tractor was droning its way across a field, a dog was barking, and the plaintive sound of gulls was overlaid by the dull thunder of the sea.

Where was she?

Propping herself up on her elbows, she frowned as she looked around the pretty bedroom. Nothing was familiar to her—except her jacket folded over the back of a rose-pink loveseat, and her strappy high heels standing beside the chair.

Then it all came rushing back. Max's fall, and her escape; the car she'd hired that had stalled just after she'd turned onto the sea road; the many futile attempts she'd made to start it again.

A shiver crept down her spine. But that still didn't explain how she came to be here, lying in a strange bed, fully clothed except for her jacket and shoes. What had happened? She put a confused hand to her head. She had to remember.

There'd been a house, she thought, her head throbbing with the effort to recall the morning's events. She'd been so relieved to find it on this lonely stretch of the coast. She'd hoped that whoever owned the house might let her use their phone to call a garage. She'd doubted she'd find a phone box this far from the village.

But the house had appeared to be empty. She remembered hearing dogs barking, and she'd been on her way back to the road when one of those big Range Rovers had pulled into the yard. Even then she'd hoped that it might be a woman driving the vehicle. At that time of the morning mothers were often employed on the school run. But the man who'd swung open the door and pushed jean-clad legs out of the car had been anything but feminine.

Matt Seton.

She swallowed, wondering if Max would have heard of him. Probably, she decided. Max had always prided himself on being familiar with every facet of the arts, and although she'd never read any of his books Seton had projected such an image of power and self-confidence that she was sure that anything he produced would be a success.

But Max was dead, she reminded herself once more, feeling a sense of panic creeping over her. In any case, she wasn't supposed to be thinking about Max right now. She was trying to work out how she came to be in Matt Seton's bedroom.

Well, maybe not his bedroom, she conceded, determinedly concentrating on the room instead of letting her thoughts numb her mind to the exclusion of anything else. She had the feeling that Matt Seton's bedroom would look nothing like this. This room was too light, too feminine. His daughter's, perhaps? He'd said he had a daughter. Did she really want to know?

Still, he had been kind to her, she acknowledged. Initially, anyway. Despite the fact that when he'd emerged from the Range Rover her primary instinct had been to run. She hadn't wanted to speak to him, hadn't wanted to put her trust—however fleetingly—into another man's hands. But common sense had won out over panic and she'd been quite proud of the way she'd handled herself then.

Until the idea of asking him for a job had occurred to her. That had been a crazy notion. She realised it now, had realised it as soon as he'd started asking questions she couldn't—or wouldn't—answer. But the thought of staying here, of blending into the landscape so that no one would find her until she wanted them to, had seemed, momentarily at least, the perfect solution.

A dog barked again. Closer at hand this time. She guessed it must be just beneath the window and she heard a man bidding it to be quiet. The man's voice was familiar, strong and attractive, and she had no difficulty in identifying it as belonging to her unwilling host.

Which brought the realisation that Matt Seton must have carried her upstairs and put her to bed. He must have removed her shoes and jacket and covered her with the quilted spread. Why? Had she fainted? Had she fallen and hit her head? No, that simply wouldn't happen. Not today. Not after...

Her bag? Alarm gripped her again. Where was her bag? Her haversack? She'd had it with her when she'd been feeling so dizzy downstairs, but she couldn't see it now. What was in it? What could Matt Seton have found if he'd looked through it? Anything incriminating? Oh, she hated that word. But was there anything to prove that her name wasn't really Sara Victor?

Throwing the coverlet aside, she swung her legs over the side of the bed and choked back a gasp of pain. Her hip throbbed abominably, and even if the room hadn't spun briefly about her she'd still have had to remain motionless until the pain subsided.

Finally it did, and, drawing up the skirt of her dress, she examined the ugly bruise that was visible below the high-cut hem of her briefs. Circles of black and blue spread out from a central contusion where ruptured blood vessels were discernible beneath the skin. It was nasty, but not life-threatening, and she touched it with cold, unsteady fingers before pulling her skirt down again.

'So you're awake!'

The voice she'd heard a few minutes before seemed to be right behind her, and she swung apprehensively towards the sound. Matt Seton was standing in the open doorway, one shoulder propped against the jamb, his eyes dark and shrewd, surveying her. How long had he been there? she wondered anxiously. Had he seen—?

She expelled an uneven breath. She was unwillingly aware that long ago, before her marriage to Max, she'd have considered Matt Seton quite a dish. Even wary and suspicious of her as he was, he still possessed the kind of animal magnetism that most women found irresistible. He wasn't handsome, though his lean hard features did have a rough appeal. But it was more than that. A combination of strength and vulnerability that she was sure had all his female acquaintances falling over themselves to help him. A subtle power that was all about sex.

She bent her head, and, as if sensing she was still not entirely recovered from her loss of consciousness, he went on, 'When did you last have a meal?'

Sara's eyes went automatically to her watch, but she saw to her dismay that it wasn't working. A crack bisected the glass and one of the hands was bent. She must have done it when she fell against the table the night before, but because until now she hadn't wanted to know what time it was she hadn't noticed.

'I—what time is it?' she asked, without answering him, and Matt pulled a wry face.

'Why? Will that change anything?' Then, when her eyes registered some anxiety, he added shortly, 'It's after one o'clock. I was about to make myself some lunch. Do you want some?'

One o'clock! Sara was horrified. She must have been unconscious for over three hours.

'You fainted,' he said, as if reading the consternation in her face. 'And then I guess, because you were exhausted, you fell asleep. Do you feel better?'

Did she? Sara had the feeling she'd never feel better again. What was going on back home? Did Hugo know Max was dead yet? Of course he must. He had been going to join them for supper after the show...

'Hello? Are you still with us?'

She must have been staring into space for several seconds, because she realised that her host had moved to the foot of the bed and was now regarding her with narrowed assessing eyes. What was he thinking? she pondered apprehensively. Why couldn't she stop giving him reasons to suspect her of God knew what? Yet, whatever he suspected, it couldn't be worse than the truth.

'I'm sorry.' She eased herself to the edge of the bed, trying not to jar her injured hip. 'When I asked to use the phone I didn't expect to make such a nuisance of myself.'

He didn't argue with her. There was no insincere attempt to put her at her ease. Just a silent acknowledgement of the statement she had made and a patient anticipation of an answer to the question he had asked earlier.

'Lunch,' he prompted her at last. 'I think we need to talk, and I'll be happier doing it when you've got some solid food inside you.'

'Perhaps I don't want to talk to you,' she retorted, getting to her feet. Without her heels he seemed that much taller, easily six feet, with a powerful muscular body that bore no resemblance to Max's more bulky frame. 'Where's my bag?'

His expression was cynical. 'There,' he said flatly, indicating a spot beside the loveseat. 'Don't worry. I haven't been rummaging through your belongings while you've been unconscious. What do you take me for?'

Sara's pale cheeks deepened with embarrassed colour. 'I—I don't know what you mean.' But she did. Max wouldn't have hesitated in using any situation to his advantage. 'I—just wanted a tissue.'

'Yeah, right.' He was sardonic. Then his brows drew together as she stepped rather stiffly into her shoes. 'Are you sure you're all right?'

'I'm fine.' But she wasn't. She'd been stiff getting out of the car, but she'd still been running on adrenalin and the ache in her hip had been bearable. Now, after resting, after giving in to her exhaustion, her senses were no longer dulled by over-active hormones and she could hardly move without wincing. 'I'm still a bit unsteady, that's all.'

Matt regarded her dourly. 'I'd say that was the understatement of the year,' he remarked, forestalling her when she would have reached for her jacket. 'You won't be needing this. Not yet,

anyway. You're going to have something to eat, even if I have
to feed you myself.'

Sara's cheeks flushed. 'You can't force me!'

'Don't make me prove it,' remarked Matt, making for the
door, her jacket looped over one shoulder. He nodded towards a
door beside the armoire. 'There's a bathroom through there. Why
don't you freshen up before the meal?' He paused. 'Oh, and there
are tissues in there, too. If you really need them.'

Sara pressed her lips together as he left the room. Once again,
he'd caught her out in a lie. But then, she was no good at lying.
She never had been. It might have been easier for her if she had.
If Max—

But she had to stop thinking about Max. Had to stop remembering how he'd humiliated and terrified her for almost three
years. Why had she stayed with him? Why had she put up with
his moods, his tempers? Because she'd been too much of a cow-
ard to break away from him? Or because she'd known what he'd
do to her and her mother if she dared to try and leave him?

And now he was dead…

Her throat felt dry, and after ensuring that Matt had left the
room she shuffled across to the bathroom. Like the bedroom, it
was predominantly peach and green in colour. Pale green bath
and basin; cream tiles with a peach flower decorating the centre;
thick peach and green towels set on a stainless steel rack.

There was a mirror above the basin and Sara examined her
reflection with critical eyes. Fortunately, her face was unmarked.
Max never left any visible signs of his cruelty, at least none that
couldn't be covered by her clothes. There had never been any
obvious signs that he was anything other than an ideal husband.
Even Hugo—gentle, bumbling Hugo—had never suspected what
a monster his brother really was. And as for her mother…

Sara trembled. She was doing it again, concentrating all her
attention on the past. She'd done what she could. She'd phoned
the emergency services before she'd fled from the apartment.
She'd ensured that Max was attended to. The only thing she
hadn't done was stay and be charged with his murder…

Expelling an unsteady breath, Sara ran some water into the
basin and washed her face and hands with the creamy soap she

found there. It was so good to get rid of the stale make-up she'd
been wearing since the night before, and, after rescuing her
haversack from the other room, she spent a few minutes applying
moisturiser to her skin. She didn't use any lipstick or mascara,
but an eyeliner was necessary to draw attention away from the
dark circles around her eyes. She looked pale, but she couldn't
help that. She had the feeling she'd never look normal again.

She found her brush and, loosening her hair, she got rid of the
tangles before plaiting it again. Then, satisfied that she'd repaired
the damage, she went back into the bedroom.

She found her hip was easier now that she was moving about
again. In a few days the bruises would disappear, as they had
done before. She'd be able to look at herself and pretend, as she
had pretended so many times before, that Max had left no scars
upon her. But the real scars went deeper, were longer lasting.
Those scars were incapable of being destroyed.

She closed her eyes for a moment, preparing herself to meet
the questions Matt Seton wasn't going to forget he hadn't had
answers to. And, before she left the room, she took off her watch
and her rings and slipped them into the bottom of her bag. One
way or another she was no longer Max's possession. She was
on her own now, and, until she decided what she was going to
do, she had to think on her feet.

There was still her mother, of course. But she doubted she
would have any sympathy for her daughter. They had never been
close, and in the older woman's eyes the only sensible thing Sara
had ever done was to marry Max Bradbury. It had always been
the same. Max could do no wrong. And, because when they'd
got married Max had moved her mother out of her run-down
house in Greenwich and into a luxury apartment in Bloomsbury,
Sara had never been able to appeal to her for help. God knew
what she'd think when she discovered Max was dead and her
daughter was missing. Sara doubted she would ever forgive her.

CHAPTER THREE

SARA looked even paler when she came downstairs, and Matt felt a heel for upsetting her. But, dammit, he hadn't been born yesterday, and it was obvious that the story she'd told him wasn't even close to the truth.

He had already beaten eggs for omelettes, and he set a bowl of freshly washed salad on the breakfast bar. Fresh coffee was simmering on the hob, and there was nearly half a bottle of Chardonnay in the fridge—a hangover from his working jag of the night before.

'Sit down,' he said, indicating the stool she had occupied before. He had considered laying the table in the dining room, but that had seemed too formal. Besides, if he had any sense he'd feed her and send her on her way without any further nonsense. It wasn't his problem if she was running away. He had been a fool to get involved. 'How do you feel?'

'Better,' she said, with another of her guarded smiles. She edged onto the stool. 'You didn't have to do this, you know.'

Yes, I did, thought Matt wryly, but he contented himself with a careless, 'No problem.' The eggs sizzled as he poured them into a hot pan. 'There's wine in the fridge, if you want it.'

'Not for me, thank you.' She was evidently trying to relax, but although she propped her elbows on the bar and looped her fingers together he could see she was on edge. Then, as if determined to behave naturally, she added, 'You said you were a writer?'

Matt cast her a sardonic glance. 'Did I say that?'

'Well, you implied as much,' she said, looking embarrassed, and he took pity on her.

'Yeah,' he agreed. 'I write.'

Her eyes widened, and he was struck anew at how lucid they were. But now that she'd removed her make-up he could see the dark shadows that surrounded them, noticed with his professional eye for observation that her skin was porcelain-fragile and almost transparent.

Who the hell was she? he wondered. What was she really doing in this part of the country? And why did he feel such an unwarranted sense of responsibility for her?

'What do you write?' she asked, apparently hoping to prevent him from asking her any more questions, and he drew a breath.

'Thrillers,' he replied at last, deciding not to elaborate. She wouldn't be interested in his background in psychology, or in the fact that the main character in his last three novels had used psychological profiling to catch his villains. Carol hadn't been. She'd thought she'd married a doctor. She'd never been interested in his writing. He tipped half the cooked eggs onto Sara's plate. 'Okay?'

She nodded her thanks for the golden-brown omelette he'd set in front of her. 'Mmm, this looks delicious.'

'So eat it,' he advised, straddling the stool opposite as he'd done before. He pulled his own plate towards him and set a board with newly sliced French bread beside them. 'Help yourself.'

He noticed how long it took her to swallow just a few mouthfuls of the omelette. She asked if she could have a glass of water and punctuated every forkful with several generous gulps so that the glass was empty long before the eggs were eaten. Much against his better judgement, Matt refilled the glass and added a handful of ice cubes from the freezer. For that she offered him a smile that for once was totally sincere.

'So—are you writing at the moment?' she asked at last, seemingly conscious of the fact that he was watching her every move. She managed to meet his eyes, if only briefly. 'It must be a fascinating occupation.'

'It's a living.' Matt helped himself to a wedge of bread and spread it thickly with butter. He offered it to her, but she declined, and, taking a bite, he chewed thoughtfully before continuing, 'I'm lucky. I enjoy it. Not all writers do, you know.'

'They don't?'

He wondered if her ingenuity was real or feigned. She certainly appeared to be interested. But then, he'd been flattered too many times before to take anything at face value. 'No,' he answered her now, forking the last of his omelette into his mouth. 'To some people, it's just a job. For me, it was a hobby long before I started to take it seriously.'

Sara looked impressed. 'It must be great to do something you really enjoy.' She cupped her chin in her hand. 'I envy you.'

'You didn't enjoy teaching, then?' suggested Matt mildly, and saw the way the colour seeped into her face at his words.

'That's different,' she said tightly. 'I meant, it must be wonderful to have a—vocation.'

'Well, I wouldn't call it that. But I know what you mean.' Matt shrugged and then directed his attention to her plate. 'Is something wrong with your eggs?'

'Oh—no.' She hurried to reassure him. 'You're a good cook. I just—er—I don't have much of an appetite, I'm afraid. I'm sorry.'

Matt collected the plates and got up to pour the coffee. Then, setting a mug of the steaming liquid in front of her, he said, 'So what are you going to do now?'

She glanced half apprehensively towards the door and he wondered if she was remembering the argument they'd had before she'd collapsed. But as far as she was concerned her vehicle was unusable. Was she thinking she would have to make other arrangements before she could continue with her journey?

'I—I suppose I should ring the garage in—where was it you said? Saviour?'

'Saviour's Bay.' Matt regarded her levelly. 'Actually, I did ring them myself.'

'You did?' The relief in her eyes made him regret the lie he'd just told her. 'What did they say? Are they sending somebody out?'

Matt ignored his twingeing conscience. 'Not until tomorrow. They're pretty strapped today.'

'Oh, no!' Her disappointment was evident. She ran slim fingers up into the hair at her temples, dragging several strands to curl about her jawline. 'God, what am I going to do now?'

He guessed the question was rhetorical, but he answered her anyway. 'You could stay here overnight,' he suggested, wondering why he was doing this. 'I have a spare room. You've just spent a couple of hours in it.'

'No!'

'Why not?' He hardened his tone. 'You were quite prepared to stay if I offered you a job. What's the difference?'

She flushed. 'That was a mistake.'

'What was?'

'Asking you for a job. I don't know what possessed me.'

'Try desperation?' he suggested flatly. 'Come on, Sara, we both know you don't have anywhere else to go. And until your car's fixed...'

She shook her head. 'I'll find a hotel. A guesthouse. Something.'

'Around here? I don't think so. Not unless you're prepared to hike several miles, as I said. And somehow, in those heels, I don't think you'd make it.'

'You don't know what shoes I've brought with me. I have a suitcase in my car—'

'No, you don't. I checked.' Matt didn't go on to add that he'd started her car, too. She must have flooded the carburettor when it had stalled and she'd tried to start it again. 'There's nothing in the boot.'

Her indignation was appealing. 'You had no right to do that.'

'No.' He agreed with her. 'But you had left the keys in the ignition. Anyone could have done the same.'

She sniffed. 'You can't force me to stay here.'

'I have no intention of forcing you to do anything,' he declared dismissively. 'And very shortly I'll be leaving to pick up my daughter from school, so you'll have every opportunity to walk out if you wish.' He shrugged. 'It's your call.'

Matt covered the distance between Seadrift and St Winifred's Primary feeling a sense of incredulity. Had he really left Sara—if that really was her name—alone in his house? After spending the last few years isolating himself from everybody but his family and the people who worked for him, had he actually encouraged a complete stranger to spend the night in his home?

Was he mad? He knew practically nothing about her, and

what he did know was definitely suspect. She had no more decided on a change of life than he had. He'd bet his last cent that she was a runaway. But from whom? And from what?

Whatever it was, he knew that it made his own misgivings about leaving her in his house groundless. She wasn't a thief. He was sure of that. Nor was she anyone's idea of a nanny, although he was prepared to believe that she hadn't been lying when she'd said she'd been a teacher. That had been the only time when there'd been real conviction in her voice. So what was she? Who was she? And what was he going to do about her?

For the present, however, he had other things to think about. Not least the fact that he had to introduce her to Rosie. He had no idea what his daughter would think of him inviting a strange woman to spend the night. Rosie might only be seven, but she could be remarkably adult on occasion, and she was bound to wonder how Sara came to be there.

To his relief, he heard the bell that marked the end of the school day as he pulled up outside the gates. He wasn't late, thank goodness. But his early arrival did mean that he had to get out of the Range Rover and be civil to the other parents who were already gathered outside the school.

'Hello, Matt.'

Gloria Armstrong, whose husband farmed several hundred acres north of Saviour's Bay, gave him a winning smile. Like several of the mothers of children in Rosie's class, she was always eager to chat with him. Matt was by no means a conceited man, but he knew these women seemed to get a disproportionate delight in using his first name. It was a pity Hester wasn't still here to run interference for him.

'Gloria,' he responded now, nodding to her and to one or two of the other parents. Thankfully, there was a handful of fathers present, too, and he was able to ally himself with them as he waited for Rosie to emerge from the school buildings.

'I hear you've had no luck in finding someone to care for Rosemary,' Gloria added, not at all daunted by his offhand greeting. Her heavily mascaraed eyes moved over his tall figure with a certain avidity. 'I wish I could do something to help.'

Yeah, right. Matt schooled his features and gave a wry smile. 'I'm sure you've got enough to do looking after those three boys of yours,' he said pleasantly. 'Not to mention your husband. How is Ron, by the way?'

Gloria's mouth turned down. 'Oh, Ron's all right,' she said dismissively. 'So long as he has his golf and his beer and his cronies, he's as happy as a pig in muck!' She grimaced. 'I sometimes think he doesn't care about me and the boys at all.'

Remembering what Rosie had said about the three boys, two of whom were in her class, Matt reserved judgement. There was no doubt they were tearaways in the making, but who was he to condemn them? He'd probably been far worse in his youth. At least if half of what his mother maintained was true.

'I imagine the farm keeps him fairly busy,' he said neutrally, wishing he could move away from her. He noticed their conversation was being observed by more than one pair of interested eyes, and the last thing he needed was for someone to mention to Ron Armstrong that he'd been seen chatting up his wife at the school gates. Despite what he'd said to Gloria, he knew her husband was a hothead and a bully. He could imagine the headlines if the other man chose to take him to task for being a womaniser.

A womaniser! Him! Matt stifled a groan. Nothing could be further from the truth. These days he was virtually celibate. The last time he'd got laid had been before Hester retired. He'd had to spend a weekend in London, visiting his agent and doing some publicity, and one of the advertising execs had come on to him. She'd been exceptionally good-looking, he recalled, but their hasty coupling in her hotel room had hardly been memorable. He'd been glad he could honestly say he was leaving London the following morning, and he'd left strict instructions with his agent that he wasn't to give his phone number to anyone...

'I wish I had a job.'

He'd forgotten Gloria was still there, but her rueful remark forced him to acknowledge her again. 'You have a job,' he said, wishing Rosie would hurry. He glanced at his watch. 'I wonder what's holding them up?'

'Who?' Gloria looked up at him with heavy-lidded eyes.

'The kids,' said Matt quellingly. Then, with some relief, 'Ah—here they are.'

'You know, I could look after Rosemary.' Gloria grabbed his arm as he would have moved away. 'At least I've had plenty of experience.'

And not just in looking after children, thought Matt drily, shaking her hand off his sleeve. For the first time he felt a little sympathy for Ron Armstrong. Perhaps he had some justification for his temper, after all.

'It's okay,' he heard himself saying now. 'I'm hoping I've found someone. She just started today, as a matter of fact.'

Gloria's full mouth took on a sulky slant. 'Well, that's news,' she said, clearly not believing him. 'I was talking to Emma Proctor yesterday morning and she didn't say anything about you hiring a nanny.'

'She doesn't know yet,' said Matt, wondering how he could have been so reckless as to say such a thing. Now he would have to ring Emma and explain the situation to her.

'Obviously not.'

Gloria sniffed, but to Matt's relief Rosie had seen him and she came barrelling out of the gate towards them.

'Daddy! Daddy!' she squealed, flinging herself into his arms. 'You came! You came!'

'I said I would, didn't I?' said Matt, swinging her round. He grinned. 'Have you had a good day?'

'Quite good—'

'Your daddy's had a better one,' put in Gloria maliciously, before Matt could perceive her intent and deflect it. 'He's found someone to look after you, Rosemary. Isn't that nice? I expect she'll be coming to meet you tomorrow.'

Rosie's eyes grew round. 'Is that true, Daddy? Has the agency sent you someone else?'

'Not exactly.' Matt could have strangled Gloria as she stood there enjoying his discomfort. Clearly she thought he was making the whole thing up and she wanted him to have to admit it. Casting her a malevolent look, he ushered Rosie away towards the Range Rover. 'I'll tell you all about it as we go home,' he promised, flicking the key fob to unlock the vehicle. 'Okay?'

'But you have found a new nanny, haven't you, Daddy?' Rosie asked, clambering, with his assistance, into the front seat. 'You weren't just saying that?'

Matt reflected again how adult Rosie was at times. He had no idea what he was going to say to her. He couldn't lie to his daughter, but equally he had to come up with a reasonable explanation of who Sara was and why she was staying at the house.

If she was still there when he got back, he acknowledged. She could have taken the keys he'd left on the counter in the kitchen and made another attempt to start her car. Once she found it was operable, she was a free agent. Whatever he thought, she'd have no reason to stay.

He sighed, fitting his keys into the ignition, and Rosie gave him a troubled look. 'What's wrong, Daddy?' she asked shrewdly. She hesitated. 'Is it because you haven't found a nanny? Did you just say that because you don't like Mrs Armstrong? 'Cos that's all right. I don't like Rupert and Nigel either.'

Rupert and Nigel! Matt raised his eyes heavenward for a moment. Nobody but Gloria Armstrong would have called those two imps of Satan *Rupert* and *Nigel*. Rosie was always telling him some story or other about what they'd got up to in the classroom, about how Mrs Sanders was forever sending them to the head teacher for extra discipline.

But grumbling about the Armstrongs wasn't going to help him now. Choosing his words with care, he said, 'A young woman did come to see me today. Not from the agency,' he added quickly, holding up a hand to prevent Rosie from interrupting. 'She's a visitor. Her car broke down at the bottom of the road and she came to ask if she could use the phone.'

Rosie's face dropped. 'So she's not a nanny?'

'No.' Matt shook his head. 'But she is going to stay with us, at least until tomorrow. So I want you to be especially nice to her.'

Rosie sniffed. 'So who is she? Why is she staying with us?'

'I've just explained,' said Matt patiently. 'Her car broke down and—she can't get it fixed until tomorrow.' May God forgive him the lie. 'She's nice. I think you'll like her.'

'What's her name?'

'Sara. Sara Victor. What do you think?'

Rosie shrugged, and Matt thought at first that she was going to reserve her opinion until she'd met their visitor. But he was wrong. His daughter was simply considering her options.

'Perhaps she'll want to stay,' she said at last, with childish optimism. 'If she likes it here, she might want to take the job.'

Matt made no response to this. He was already regretting having to discuss Sara's arrival with her. But then, he'd known he'd have to give some explanation to his daughter. Unfortunately Gloria Armstrong had precipitated the event.

It seemed to take for ever to get back to Saviour's Bay. Now that she knew about Sara, Rosie wasn't interested in talking about her day at school. She just turned the conversation back to Sara, and he eventually gave up trying to talk about anything else.

She wanted to know Sara's age, what she looked like, where she came from. If she was on holiday, what was wrong with her car? The questions came thick and fast, and Matt dreaded getting back to Seadrift and finding that Sara had gone. He didn't know what he'd tell his daughter if that happened. And, however slight the association was, he knew Rosie would be very disappointed, too.

Would he be disappointed?

That was a question he chose not to ask himself. Yet he knew he was curious about Sara as well. From a professional point of view, he assured himself firmly. As a psychological case, she interested him greatly. But that was all it was, he told himself. He had no interest in her as a woman at all. The days when he'd allowed his hormones to govern his actions were long gone. Any relationships he had were short and rarely sweet. Which suited him.

It was something of a relief to find that the hired Ford was still parked where Sara had left it. If it wouldn't have caused complications that he chose not to get into right now he'd have shifted it inside his own gates. But towing it would require her assistance, and she might just be tempted to try and start it herself.

'Is that her car?' asked Rosie, peering over her shoulder as they drove up the private road to the house. 'What's wrong with it?'

'I've already told you. I don't know,' said Matt, disliking the untruth almost as much as his own behaviour. 'Can you sit still? We're almost there.'

'Where is she?'

Rosie was still full of questions, and Matt expelled a weary breath. 'I expect she's in the sitting room,' he said shortly, hoping Sara hadn't been invading the rest of the house. He didn't think it was likely. She'd seemed quite happy in the spacious sitting room, with its broad windows that overlooked the sweep of the bay.

Rosie had her door open as soon as he stopped the car, jumping down onto the paved forecourt, dragging her canvas bag behind her. Scurrying round the corner of the building, she briefly disappeared from view, but Matt could hear the dogs barking as she reached the back door.

Striding after her, he saw her stop outside the dogs' compound and open the gate. Then, after bending to fuss over the two animals, she turned to enter the house. 'Don't,' yelled Matt, but it was too late. Rosie had already opened the door, and the retrievers bounded boisterously after her.

By the time he reached the kitchen Rosie and the dogs had disappeared, but he could hear them rampaging into the sitting room, barking again. There was shouting, mostly from Rosie, and laughter, which he was amazed to identify as coming from his visitor, and when he arrived at the sitting room doorway he was confronted by a scene he'd never expected. Sara was down on her knees, fussing over the animals, and Rosie was standing watching her with a look of delighted anticipation on her small face.

It was a long time since he'd seen Rosie so animated with someone other than himself, and he felt a twinge of guilt for neglecting her, for making her a hostage to the life he chose to lead. It hadn't been so bad when they'd had Hester. She'd compensated for the extended family Rosie didn't have. But since Hester had retired Rosie had had only his parents to rely on. And, apart from the fact that they lived in Cumbria, they were enjoying their retirement too much for him to inflict a lively seven-year-old on them very often.

But Rosie was evidently enjoying herself now, and he suspected Sara was, too, though she sobered a little and scrambled to her feet when he appeared. He noticed she'd discarded the strappy shoes in favour of going barefoot, and he wondered why he was suddenly struck with the fact of how sexy bare feet could be.

'I'm sorry,' he said, distracting himself. Collecting his wayward thoughts, he indicated the dogs. 'I couldn't stop Rosie from letting them in.'

'That's okay.' Sara brushed her skirt, dispersing a fine cloud of dog hairs into the atmosphere. 'I had to meet them again sometime.'

'Sara, don't you like Hubble and Bubble?' demanded Rosie indignantly, and Matt gave an exasperated sigh. He could do without this.

'Not everyone's as mad about dogs as you are, Rosie,' he retorted, his tone sharper than it might have been because of his own reactions. He forced himself to look briefly in Sara's direction before adding, 'And I don't recall your being given permission to call our guest by her first name. I think you should apologise.'

Rosie flushed at the reproof, but before Matt could feel any remorse Sara intervened. 'I don't mind,' she said, smiling at the little girl. 'What was it you called the dogs? Hubble and Bubble?' And, at Rosie's nod, 'Well, I suppose they introduced us, didn't they?' She held out her hand towards the child. 'I'm very pleased to meet—all of you.'

Rosie was completely won over. Matt could see that. Any concerns she'd voiced on the way home from school were totally dispelled by the warmth of Sara's smile.

Conversely, Matt wasn't sure now that that was what he wanted. It was one thing feeling sorry for the woman, and quite another seeing his daughter responding to her undoubted charm. He knew absolutely nothing about her, he reminded himself irritably. He certainly didn't know why *he'd* invited her to stay.

'I'm pleased to meet you,' Rosie was saying delightedly, casting a triumphant glance up at her father. 'Daddy says you're going to stay with us. I hope you do.'

'Oh—well, it's just for one night,' Sara murmured a little awkwardly. 'It's very kind of your father to invite me.'

She didn't know the half of it, thought Matt, raking long fingers through his hair, but before he could respond Rosie jumped in again. 'But you do like it here, don't you?' she asked. 'Are you on holiday? Or are you looking for a job?'

Now Matt saw it was Sara's turn to look disconcerted. 'I—I haven't decided,' she said at last, a faint flush tingeing the skin of her throat. The unsuitable voile dress exposed a fair amount of her neck and throat, he noticed, and, as if conscious of this, she crossed her arms at her midriff, one hand seeking to protect herself from his eyes. 'This is a very—beautiful place.' She glanced towards the windows, the tip of her tongue touching her parted lips. 'I think you're very lucky to live here.'

Matt found to his annoyance that his eyes were following her tongue's sensual exploration. And he felt impatient with himself for being so immature. For God's sake, he was a grown man, not a schoolboy. What was there about this woman that affected him so?

'That's what Daddy always says,' exclaimed Rosie now, rather wistfully, and Matt wondered if he was depriving his daughter of a social life. Seadrift was remote. There was no getting away from it. But he resented the thought that a stranger should bring it to mind.

'I'm sure he's right,' Sara murmured, no doubt for her own reasons, he thought savagely. He didn't need her endorsement. In fact, he needed nothing from her, he thought irritably. She bent to pat the two retrievers, exposing the dusky hollow of her cleavage. 'You probably couldn't keep these two rascals if you lived in a town.'

'Do you live in a town?' asked Rosie. Then, without pausing, 'Would you like to live at the coast?'

Matt stiffened. 'Rosie!' he said warningly, half afraid he knew what was coming. But he couldn't stop her. It was too late.

''Cos Daddy's looking for someone to come and look after me,' she explained eagerly. 'You wouldn't have to do much. Just take me to school and stuff. You wouldn't really be a nanny,' she ran on, ''cos I'm too old for that. But you could live here—couldn't she, Daddy? And then I wouldn't be always getting in your way when you're working, like you said.'

CHAPTER FOUR

SARA didn't want to feel any sympathy for Matt Seton, but she couldn't help it. She saw the look of anguish that crossed his lean tanned features at the child's careless words. He obviously cared deeply about his daughter, and it hurt him to hear her describe the way she thought he thought about her. She sensed he was fostering all the remorse of a single father who was obliged to employ strangers to care for his child while he earned them both a living.

But she also glimpsed a thread of anger in the gaze he directed towards her, and she wondered if he thought she had engineered Rosie's innocent invitation.

'I—' She strove to find an explanation for not accepting the position that wouldn't offend the little girl. 'It's very kind of you, Rosie—'

'But Miss Victor is heading off tomorrow,' put in the child's father harshly, before Sara could finish, and, despite the fact that she'd been about to say something similar, Sara felt her hackles rise at his callous dismissal. 'Besides,' he went on, rather maliciously, she thought, 'I'm sure our visitor would find our way of life very dull.'

Rosie looked crestfallen now. 'Would you?' she asked, her dark eyes, so like her father's, gazing up at Sara in mute appeal. Sara thought it would have taken a harder heart than hers to resist her, but once again Matt Seton saved her the trouble.

'Of course she would,' he essayed flatly. 'Now—shall we get these animals out of here before they shed any more hair?'

Rosie's lip jutted. 'If you say so.'

'I do say so,' declared her father inflexibly, ushering the two retrievers into the hall. 'If you'll excuse us, Miss Victor?'

It was a perfunctory enquiry at best, and Sara expelled a breath before lifting her shoulders in a conciliatory gesture. 'Is there anything I can do?' she asked, deciding there was no point in pretending that she could go against his wishes, however enthusiastic Rosie might be.

Matt Seton paused in the doorway. 'You're a guest,' he said simply. 'If you'll excuse me, I'll go and see what my house-keeper has left for our evening meal.'

Sara took a couple of steps after him. 'It's early yet,' she protested. Then, with inspiration, 'Don't these dogs need exercising or something? I—Rosie and I could take them for a walk.'

'I don't think so.'

His cold denial came only seconds before Rosie's, 'Oh, why not, Daddy? We often take the dogs out after I get home from school.'

'*We* do,' he said, emphasising the personal pronoun. 'Be-sides—' he gave Sara another impatient look '—Miss Victor doesn't have any suitable footwear.'

'I don't need shoes on the beach,' she exclaimed, the idea growing on her. She found the prospect of running along the shoreline, paddling in the cool waters of this northerly sea, more and more appealing. She couldn't run away from her troubles. She knew that. But perhaps this was a way to escape from them for a while. 'We wouldn't go far. I promise.'

'I'm sorry.'

He was adamant, and her spirits plummeted. But how could she blame him really? She hadn't exactly behaved responsibly this far.

'You could come with us, Daddy.'

Clearly Rosie wasn't prepared to accept his refusal without an attempt to change his mind, and Sara sensed he was torn by the knowledge that he was on the point of disappointing her once again.

'Rosie,' he began, a little wearily, but she evidently sensed he was weakening.

'Please, Daddy,' she begged, clutching his hand. 'You need the exercise, too. You're always saying so. Come on. It'll be fun.'

Matt looked as if that was the last word he'd have used to

describe the proposed outing, and, judging by the look he cast in her direction, Sara guessed he blamed her entirely.

But this time he wasn't prepared to risk another rift with his daughter. 'Well,' he began slowly, 'perhaps for half an hour—'

He wasn't allowed to finish. Rosie squealed with delight, throwing her arms around his hips and hugging him tightly. Matt's hands were gentle on her shoulders, but over his daughter's head his eyes told Sara a different story. However, she wasn't prepared to deal with his resentment; not now. Glancing out of the window again, she saw that although the sun was still fighting with the clouds a stiff breeze was flattening the grass on the cliff top. She would wear her jacket, she thought, concentrating on the needs of the moment. There was no point in risking a chill, however bleak her future looked at present.

They left the house through the kitchen, but this time they turned away from the front of the house. Instead, they followed a grassy path through a walled plot where wallflowers grew in wild profusion and rambling roses covered a latticed trellis, their scent evocative on the afternoon air.

The dogs bounded ahead, their flowing tails wagging excitedly as they led the way across the cliffs to where a rocky path meandered down to the beach. They were obviously used to this walk, and although they occasionally turned back to ensure that their human companions were following they needed no encouragement.

'This is lovely, isn't it, Daddy?' exclaimed Rosie, who had thrown off her school blazer and was jumping up and down beside the adults. 'Aren't you glad you came now?'

Matt's mouth compressed for a moment, before the smile he reserved for his daughter appeared again. 'I guess,' he said drily. Then, with a disturbing look at Sara's feet, 'Are you sure you want to go down here without shoes?'

Sara had been wondering the same thing, but his sardonic words hardened her resolve. 'I'm sure,' she said, going ahead as if she was used to negotiating rocky paths in her bare feet every day. She started down with a confidence she didn't feel. 'No problem.'

In fact, her feet felt as if they'd encountered every sharp stone on the path by the time she reached the bottom. It was only by a supreme effort of will that she stopped herself from crying out at times. Still, the soft sand was balm to her bruised soles, and she strode off towards the water with real enthusiasm.

After a few moments Rosie joined her, and then, after assuring herself that Sara was all right, she raced off in pursuit of the dogs. With a feeling of inevitability Sara realised she was going to have to be content with Matt Seton's company, and she was hardly surprised when he said drily, 'Not as easy as it looked, was it?'

'I'm not as fragile as you seem to think,' she retorted, catching her breath when she inadvertently trod into a pool of cold water. Then, forcing her mind away from her own problems, she took a deep breath and said, 'I never realised there were still untouched beaches like this in England.' She looked about her. 'It's amazing!'

'Oh, Robinson Crusoe has nothing on us,' remarked Matt, matching her mood. 'Despite the isolation, it's a good place to live.'

'I can believe it.' She sighed, and then caught her breath again as an errant wave drenched her ankles. 'What made you choose it?'

'Its remoteness from London?' he suggested. And then, as if aware that his answer had raised more questions, he went on, 'No, I am from this area originally. I guess that's why it appeals to me.'

'But you used to live in London?'

Her audacity surprised her, and she was quite prepared for him to remain silent. But then he said, 'For my sins. When I left university it was the place to be.' He paused. 'How about you, Miss Victor? Are you a runaway from London, too?'

'You don't run away from places,' she retorted recklessly, and was instantly aware that she'd aroused his interest.

'No, you don't,' he agreed. 'Which begs the question, who are you running away from?' He waited a beat. 'Who—or what?'

That was too close for comfort, and, taking advantage of the fact that he was still wearing his shoes, she trod further into the water. It was cold, and her skin feathered instinctively, but anything was better than fencing words with a man who was proving far too perceptive for her peace of mind.

To her relief, Rosie provided a distraction. Seeing that Sara was in the water, albeit only up to her ankles, she came running back to join them, peeling off her own shoes and socks with obvious intent.

'No, Rosie.' Her father grabbed the little girl before she could scamper into the water. 'It's too cold yet,' he insisted, ignoring her protests. 'Miss Victor was just coming out—weren't you, Miss Victor?'

Sara didn't have a lot of choice. Besides, the water was proving much cooler than she'd anticipated. 'That's right,' she said, avoiding his eyes in favour of the child's. She stepped out onto the damp sand and smiled at Rosie. 'Look, I've got goosebumps.'

Rosie struggled to get over her disappointment. 'Have you?' she asked doubtfully, and Sara squatted down beside her to help her put her shoes on again.

'Everywhere,' she assured the little girl, indicating her wrists and bare legs, and knew the instant when Matt Seton joined his daughter in assessing her appearance.

She was immediately conscious of the fact that the hem of her skirt had fallen back to mid-thigh, exposing her knees and several inches of flesh above them. Matt's eyes seemed to touch her skin and, although she knew it was crazy, she felt that appraisal deep within her bones.

Heat, strong and totally inappropriate, flooded her chilled limbs, and she couldn't wait to get to her feet and put some distance between them. She wasn't attracted to this man, she told herself fiercely. She couldn't be. Not in her present situation. After the way Max had treated her, she'd always believed she'd never want to get involved with any man ever again, and for all she knew Matt Seton might be just like him. After all, he looked bigger and stronger, and therefore more dangerous.

When she tried to get to her feet again, however, her legs gave way under her. Her bruised hip screamed with pain when she tried to straighten it, and she sank down onto her knees in total humiliation.

But, the damp sand had barely had time to coat her skin before hands fastened about her upper arms and helped her up again. Favouring her uninjured leg, she managed to support her weight with an effort, and even managed a light tone as she said, 'Sorry about that. I must have lost my balance.'

Matt let her go with obvious reluctance. 'Are you sure that was all it was?' he asked, and she could tell from his expression that he distrusted her story. 'I think we'd better be getting back,' he added, whistling to the dogs, and she was grateful he was giving her time to pull herself together.

'I fall over all the time,' said Rosie comfortingly, trying to reassure her. 'Do you want to hold my hand?'

'Thanks.' Sara forced a smile, even though she knew her face must look pinched. 'I think I'm all right now.'

And it was true. She could put her weight on her injured hip again now. Not heavily, of course, and not with the freedom with which she'd come down the cliff path. But, as before, it got easier as she moved forward, and she faced the climb with only a small amount of trepidation.

Even so, going up the cliff was much different from coming down. Each step required an effort, and although Rosie surged ahead, Matt insisted on following behind. She didn't truly believe he was doing it because he got some pleasure out of watching her struggles, but she was very relieved when she reached the top.

She longed to sink down onto the grass then, and allow her aching limbs to relax, but she didn't dare. She had to keep going until she got back to the house at least. Even then she had to remain on her guard. Or Matt might get even more suspicious. She already knew he was not an easy man to deceive.

Back at the house, with the dogs corralled in their compound in the yard, Rosie was sent to change her clothes and Sara asked if it would be all right if she went to her room. 'I'd like to have a wash,' she said, picturing the bed where she had rested earlier with real longing. 'If you don't mind.'

Matt regarded her consideringly. 'Why don't you have a bath?' he suggested. 'I expect you're feeling quite stiff.'

Sara sucked in a breath. 'Why do you say that?' she demanded, and he lifted his shoulders in a careless gesture.

'Well, you have had a long drive,' he pointed out mildly, and she dipped her eyes to hide the relief that rose in her face.

'I—I see,' she said, glancing about her for the haversack which she'd left behind when they went out. She managed a slight smile. 'I suppose you're right.'

'Why else would your legs give out on you?' he queried, and she wondered just how innocent his remarks really were.

'I—they didn't give out,' she protested. 'I told you. I lost my balance.'

'I know what you told me,' he returned, taking off the cream sweater he'd pulled on over his black tee shirt when they'd left the house. He smoothed his ruffled hair with long-fingered hands. 'Okay. Have it your own way. But I'd still get in the bath if I were you.'

Sara straightened up. 'I might do that.'

'Be my guest.'

She was aware that he watched her as she left the kitchen. She didn't know what he was thinking, but she knew she hadn't done anything to improve his opinion of her by collapsing on the beach.

It was surprisingly easy to find the room where she'd rested earlier. She could hear Rosie clattering about in her room, which was apparently further along the galleried landing, but Sara went into her own room and closed the door behind her. Then, sinking down onto the side of the bed, she allowed her body to sag with relief. Exhaustion rounded her shoulders and she allowed her wrists to fall loosely between her knees.

Had he believed her? Or did he suspect that there was more to her conduct than a simple stiffness in her spine? No doubt he had a computer. He'd need one for his writing. Was he even now combing the Internet for any story that might match her unconvincing explanation?

She looked for her watch and then remembered that she'd taken it off before lunch. It was broken anyway, so it wouldn't have been any good to her. Besides, she knew it was nearly five o'clock. She'd seen a clock in the kitchen. Almost a whole day had passed since she'd left the apartment. She'd been a widow for almost twenty-four hours. She shivered. Oh, God, what was she going to do?

The effort required in taking a bath wasn't particularly appealing now, but she guessed the hot water might soothe her aches and pains. Somehow she had to get through the next fifteen hours without breaking down. When Matt left to take Rosie to school the following morning she'd ask him to give her a lift into Saviour's Bay. With a bit of luck her car might be repaired by lunchtime, and then she'd be free to move on.

But where?

And what if Matt wouldn't let her go?

But she wouldn't think like that, she told herself severely. He couldn't keep her here by force and, despite what he'd said before, she didn't think he'd report her to the authorities. Not without knowing who she was. He wasn't that kind of man. She didn't know how she knew that, but she did.

The corner bath filled quickly. She found some pine-scented bath gel in a glass cabinet over the sink and added a squeeze of fragrance to the water. Steam rose, warm and scented, into her nostrils, and she felt a twinge of anticipation at the prospect of feeling clean again. One day at a time, Sara, she told herself encouragingly. She had to believe that she'd get through this.

It was hard to hold on to that thought when she took off her clothes, however. With the removal of her dress it was impossible to avoid the many bruises and contusions colouring her pale skin. She looked as if she'd been in a fist fight, she mused bitterly, and of course she had. But there had only ever been one real contender.

Yet Max was dead and she was alive...

The incredible truth couldn't be denied and she sagged weakly against the basin. She hadn't meant for him to die, she insisted painfully. But who was going to believe her now?

For so long she'd accepted that her hands were tied, that there was nothing she could do to change things. Even without the threats Max had made against her mother, she'd known he would never let her go. He'd told her so many times. And she'd believed him. God knew, she'd had every reason to believe his threats before.

So what had happened last night? How had the victim suddenly become the hunted? She'd had no notion that anything different was about to happen. She'd been too busy defending herself to anticipate that help might come from a totally unexpected source.

She swallowed the sickly feeling that surged into her throat at the memory. She saw Max raising his hand towards her, saw herself falling against the corner table on the landing of their duplex apartment. Even now her hip throbbed in memory of the agonising pain that had stunned her at the impact. She remembered rolling herself into a ball, arms curled over her head in mute acceptance of the boot that would surely follow—but it hadn't happened. Instead, Max had lost his balance. He'd tripped, swearing as he'd stumbled over her crumpled body, and, unable to save himself, had fallen headlong down the stairs.

Another wave of nausea gripped her. It had been an accident, she assured herself now, as she'd assured herself then. If she'd rolled against his legs, if she'd caused him to lose his balance, it hadn't been deliberate. If he hadn't hit her, if he hadn't caused her to fall across the head of the stairs, she wouldn't have provided an obstacle. She'd never dreamt that he might trip over her; that he'd break his neck as he fell.

But it had happened. She could hear Max's voice in her ears, hear the frantic cries he'd made as he'd tried desperately to save himself. He hadn't given up without a struggle. She'd heard the scratching of his fingernails against the banister, the creaking of the wood beneath his weight. And then the awful thudding sound as his body pitched forward, no longer aggressive, out of his control.

An accident.

She sucked in a breath. That was what it had been. When she'd scurried down the stairs to where he was lying in the foyer of the apartment she'd had no other thought in her mind than to assure him she was sorry, so sorry, for what had happened.

But he'd been lying still, so very still, and she'd guessed at once that it was hopeless. She'd attempted to revive him. She'd even put her trembling mouth over his cold one and tried to breathe air into his lungs. He hadn't responded. That was when she'd called the emergency services. That was when she'd known she had to get away.

She'd realised how it would look to a stranger. Realised that she was virtually admitting her guilt. But it was no good. No one was going to believe it was just an accident. Men like Max, men who were fit and strong, didn't just fall down a flight of stairs without provocation. And if they arrested her, if they examined her and saw what he'd had done to her. Well, she was afraid her battered body would prove her guilt.

She expelled the breath she had hardly been aware she was holding, and then almost jumped out of her skin when someone knocked on the bathroom door.

Immediately she sprang to brace a shoulder against the panels, terrified that whoever it was out there was going to open the door and see her naked flesh. She suspected that Matt Seton was still curious about her. And if he glimpsed—

But she stifled the thought, saying instead, 'What do you want?' in a voice that sounded annoyingly tremulous even to her.

'You okay?'

It was Matt, and unreasonable irritation gripped her. 'Why shouldn't I be?'

'No reason, I guess. Except that you've been in there for over half an hour and I haven't heard a sound since the water stopped running,' he replied mildly. 'I wondered if you'd fallen asleep? That can be dangerous, you know.'

She gulped. 'Are you spying on me?'

'Hardly.' His tone had hardened, and she couldn't honestly blame him. He'd been concerned, that was all. Something she wasn't used to. 'Anyway,' he went on, 'supper will be ready in about an hour, so don't hurry. You've got plenty of time.'

Sara pressed her hot cheek against the wood. 'Thanks.'

'No sweat.' The harshness had left his voice. 'Just don't drown yourself, okay?'

Her lips quivered. 'Okay.'

'Good.'

She heard him leaving the bedroom, heard the outer door slam behind him, and breathed a little more easily again. But she couldn't help the frisson of pleasure she felt at the knowledge that he'd been worried about her. It was so long since anyone had cared about her in that way. Hugo had treated her with affection, it was true, but she'd always known that in any real confrontation he would always take Max's side. He was his brother, after all, and without Max's support his acting career would very likely have slid back into oblivion where it had begun.

But she had to stop thinking about Max, she thought fiercely, checking that the door was securely closed before crossing the room again and easing herself into the bath. There was no lock on the door, but she found she trusted Matt Seton not to come in without an invitation. As for Rosie: she seemed like the kind of little girl who would follow her father's example. Abandoning herself to anything but the reassuring embrace of the water, Sara sat down.

She winced as its heat probed the tender places of the hip and thigh she'd injured when she fell. Even sitting on the hard enamel was painful at first, but after a few minutes the warmth acted as an analgesic and she was able to relax. She leaned back against the side of the bath and closed her eyes.

Goodness, that felt good. She couldn't remember the last time she'd had a bath. These days taking a shower was so much quicker and easier. Besides, she avoided spending too much time in the bathroom. Without her clothes she felt that much more vulnerable, and it wasn't above Max to take advantage of it. She'd dreaded those occasions when he'd stepped into the shower with her and—

Her eyes jerked open. She must stop reliving the past. Eventually what had happened was going to catch up with her, but for now she had to think of something else. She had to think about herself, think of what she was going to do tomorrow. The future stretched ahead of her, uncharted. And, however shameful the admission, she was glad Max was never going to be able to hurt her again.

By the time she got out of the bath she was feeling infinitely more human. She dried herself on one of the large towels from the rack and then, after a moment's hesitation, wrapped herself in the cream towelling bathrobe she found hanging on the back of the door. She wondered if Matt would mind if she wore the robe for a couple of hours. Then she could wash and dry her bra and panties. The expensive scraps of silk and lace that Max had bought for her would need no artificial drying, and she'd feel infinitely fresher wearing clean underwear tomorrow.

When she opened the door into the bedroom, however, she discovered that, as well as checking on her well-being, Matt had also left a pile of clothes on the bed. Sara's eyes widened in amazement when she discovered a cellophane-wrapped package of bikini briefs beneath what were obviously his chambray shirt and sweat pants. The shirt and sweat pants were freshly laundered, but it was obvious that the package containing the briefs hadn't been opened. Where had they come from? she wondered. He hadn't mentioned a girlfriend. But a man like him was bound to have women friends. Hadn't he been speaking to one of them—Emma—earlier on?

Still, the idea that he might have contacted one of his girlfriends for help didn't sit well with her, and she caught her lower lip between her teeth as she turned the packet over in her hands. And discovered that the label indicated that they were suitable for a nine- to ten-year-old!

Rosie! she thought incredulously, a gulp of laughter escaping her. They had obviously been bought for Rosie, but just as obviously they were too big for her. Ripping open the cellophane, Sara pulled them out and examined them more closely. Made of white cotton, they looked plain and practical, and, although they'd probably be a tight fit, she thought they'd do very well.

A feeling of gratitude filled her, and with it a sense of shame at her own presumption. Matt was trying to help her; that was obvious. She had to stop believing that all men were like Max.

They weren't. He had been the exception. Was it evil to be glad he was finally out of her life?

The briefs were barely decent, but Sara didn't care. With Matt's sweat pants bulking around her thighs, and the ends of his shirt tied at her waist, she looked anything but provocative. He'd also left a pair of sports socks, which she found worked equally well as slippers. After she'd rinsed out her own bra and panties, and hung them on the radiator in the bathroom to dry, all that was left for her to do was brush out her hair and plait it again. She was sitting at the dressing table, securing it with an elasticated band, when there was another knock at her door.

She stiffened. She couldn't help it. Old habits die hard, she thought, taking a deep breath and calling, 'Who is it?'

'It's me. Rosie.' The little girl needed no further bidding before opening the door and putting her head round it. 'Can I come in?'

Sara found herself smiling. 'It looks as if you are in,' she remarked mildly. 'But, yes. Come in. What can I do for you?'

Rosie entered the room, revealing that she'd changed out of her school clothes into cut-off jeans and a pink tee shirt. She had evidently washed her face, too, though Sara could see the telltale smears of what appeared to be chocolate around her mouth. But she looked sweet and wholesome, and Sara wanted to hug her.

'Daddy says supper will be ready in ten minutes,' she declared, regarding her father's guest with interest. 'Are those Daddy's clothes?'

'Yes.' Sara nodded. 'He was kind enough to lend them to me.' She got up from the stool. 'How do I look?'

'We—ll.' Rosie was thoughtful. 'They look a bit big,' she confessed at last. Then, glancing about her, 'Don't you have any clothes of your own?'

'Not here,' replied Sara, determinedly suppressing thoughts of where the rest of her clothes were. 'Oh, and your father gave me these.' She held up the packet that had contained the bikini briefs. 'I hope you don't mind.'

'Oh, no!' Rosie giggled. 'Daddy's Aunt Margaret sent them

last Christmas. She's ever so old, and Daddy says her eyes aren't as good as they used to be.'

'Ah.' Sara screwed the packet into a ball, preparatory to taking it downstairs to throw away. 'Well, I'm very grateful for that.'

'Do they really fit you?' asked Rosie, staring at her critically, as if trying to imagine how they might look on an adult, and Sara grimaced.

'Just about,' she answered, a mischievous grin tugging at her lips. 'Shall we go down?'

Rosie hesitated. 'Have you changed your mind? About staying, I mean? I wish you would.'

Sara sighed. 'Rosie—'

''Cos Daddy really needs someone. We slept in this morning, and I was nearly late for school.'

Sara shook her head. 'I don't think we should be having this conversation, Rosie.'

'Why not?'

'Because—because, like your Daddy said, I've got to leave tomorrow.'

Rosie's lips pursed. 'Don't you like it here, either?'

'Of course I do.' Sara wished she didn't have to lie to the child. 'I think you're very lucky to live so close to the sea.'

'Most people don't.'

'Well, I do.'

'Then—'

'I think we should go down for supper,' Sara insisted firmly. She pulled a face at her reflection, knowing the little girl could see her. 'I just hope your father isn't expecting any visitors tonight.'

CHAPTER FIVE

MATT came awake slowly, staring up at the ceiling that was striped with bars of sunlight. He'd left the window open the night before, he remembered, and the slats of the blind were moving in the breeze.

He often left his window open. He liked to come awake to the muted roar of the sea. The constant movement of the tides gave him a feeling of constancy, a sense of knowing that in this world not everything was subject to change.

So why did he have such a feeling of unease this morning? he wondered, pushing the sheet back to his waist and running an exploratory hand over the rough pelt of hair that angled down to his navel and beyond. And then he remembered his uninvited visitor. Sara Victor, if that really was her name. And why should he care, anyway? She was leaving this morning. When he got back from taking Rosie to school he'd pretend to check her car and miraculously find that it was working. Then she'd have no excuse to hang about any longer, and he could get back to doing the job he loved.

Only it wasn't quite that simple. Rosie had taken an instant liking to her, which was unusual in itself. Since Hester had retired the little girl had been introduced to many of the would-be nannies who had turned up at his door, and she hadn't been impressed with any of them. Granted, most of the younger ones hadn't wanted to live in the area, but even those who had had left a lot to be desired so far as Rosie was concerned.

He'd agreed with her for the most part. He didn't want Rosie's life controlled by either a bimbo or a martinet. And, although he'd made it clear that he wasn't interested in any attachment, he'd always been aware of the dangers inherent in having a younger woman living in his house.

And now Rosie had formed an attachment of her own.

He'd seen it happening, of course. All last evening he'd been forced to watch his daughter falling more and more deeply under Sara's unconscious spell. And it was unconscious. He knew that. Sara hadn't set out to entrance the little girl; she just couldn't help doing so.

She had the knack of drawing Rosie out of herself. Without talking down to her, she was able to put herself on the child's level, and Rosie had responded in kind. Matt hadn't been aware that his daughter was missing anything until he'd heard her discussing her dolls' outfits with Sara. What did he know of women's fashions, or of the most attractive shades of lipstick and nail varnish? He hadn't even known Rosie knew about such things until she'd produced a bottle of some glittery substance, which had apparently come as a free gift with one of the pre-teen magazines he'd bought for her, and proceeded to paint Sara's nails with it.

When he'd protested that Miss Victor couldn't possibly want her nails painted that particular shade of pink, Sara had insisted she didn't mind.

'It's okay,' she'd assured him lightly. 'It washes off.' Then she'd given a wry smile. 'At least I hope it does.' She'd held up her hand and wiggled her fingers. 'Do you like it?'

Matt didn't remember what he'd said. Whatever it was, it had made no lasting impression on him. What he did remember was that she disturbed him; that he'd been far too aware of her as a woman ever since she'd appeared downstairs wearing his old chambray shirt and sweats.

When he'd left the clothes on her bed he'd never dreamt that he'd have such a powerful reaction to her wearing them. But the knowledge that she'd obviously not been wearing a bra had aroused the most unsettling images in his head. He'd found himself wondering whether she'd bothered to put on the briefs he'd found in Rosie's drawer. Or had they been too small for her? The possibility that she might be naked beneath the baggy trousers was all he'd needed to fuel his imagination.

He reluctantly recalled how he'd felt when Rosie had crept into his room after he'd retired, begging him to ask Sara to stay. 'Just for a few days, Daddy,' she'd entreated him appealingly, and, although Matt had told her no, he couldn't help the treacherous thought that employing Sara could be beneficial to both of them.

But that wasn't an option. Rolling onto his stomach, Matt was aware that his morning erection hadn't subsided. Hard and insistent, it throbbed against his stomach, and he was irritably aware that it was thinking about his house guest that had caused it. It was all too easy to imagine how delightful it would have been to strip the sweat pants from her and sate his burning flesh between her thighs. He could almost feel those long slim legs wrapped around his waist, her firm breasts crushed against his chest. When he brought them both to a shuddering climax she'd sob her gratitude in his ear, whispering how much she'd wanted him, how amazing their lovemaking had been...

'Are you awake, Daddy?'

The stage whisper sent Matt's senses reeling. And aroused an immediate feeling of self-disgust. Dammit, what was wrong with him? he asked himself irritably. What on earth was there about Sara Victor that aroused the kind of fantasies he hadn't had since he was a teenager? It wasn't as if she was incredibly beautiful. She was good-looking, yeah, but she was no super-model. Nor did she behave in a way designed to provoke such a reaction. If he was feeling in need of a woman it was his fault, not hers. He needed to get laid, and quick. Before he was tempted to do something they would all regret.

But right now Rosie took precedence, and, rolling onto his side to face her, he contrived a smile. 'Hey, sweetheart,' he said, with what he thought was admirable self-restraint. 'What are you doing up so early?'

Rosie was hovering by the door. In cropped Winnie the Pooh pyjamas, her cheeks pink, her hair tousled, she looked adorable, and Matt thought again how lucky he was to have her. 'Can I come in?' she asked, glancing over her shoulder half apprehensively. 'I want to talk to you.'

Matt compressed his lips. 'That sounds ominous,' he remarked drily, guessing the topic. 'Why do I get the feeling that I'm not going to like what you have to say?'

'Oh, Daddy!' Rosie took his response as an invitation to join him and came to climb onto the bottom of the bed. Then, realising she'd left the door open, she scrambled down again and went to close it. After she'd resumed her position against the footboard, she declared urgently, 'It's about Sara.'

Matt had assumed as much, but he didn't let on. Instead, he pushed himself up against his pillows and regarded his daughter enquiringly. 'Don't you mean Miss Victor?'

'She said I could call her Sara,' protested Rosie at once. 'Last night. When she came to say goodnight. She said that calling her Miss Victor made her feel as if she was back in school again.' She paused. 'Did you know she used to be a school-teacher, Daddy?'

Matt blew out a breath. So she'd told Rosie she used to teach, had she? He would like to think it had just been a casual admission, but he couldn't help wondering if she'd said it deliberately. To persuade him that she hadn't been lying about that, at least. Or to get the child to speak to him on her behalf.

'I believe she said something about it,' he admitted now. 'So—is that all you wanted to tell me?'

'Hardly,' said Rosie indignantly. 'I just wondered if you knew, that's all.'

'Well, I do.' Matt arched his dark brows. 'What else is new?'

'Daddy!' Rosie looked red-faced now. 'Give me a chance! I can't think of everything all at once.'

'Okay.' Matt contained his amusement. 'It must be something serious to get you out of bed before seven o'clock.'

'Oh, Daddy.' Rosie gazed at him impatiently. 'You know what I'm going to say.' She paused. 'Why can't you ask Sara to stay?'

Matt sighed. 'We talked about this last night, Rosie.'

'But you need a nanny. You said so yourself. Or I mean I do. Why can't it be Sara?'

'Rosie—'

'Please!'

'Look,' he said, trying to reason with her. 'We know nothing about Sara. We don't even know where she came from.'

'Then ask her,' said Rosie practically. 'I'm sure she'd tell you if you did. She told me I was very lucky to live by the seaside. She said that when she was just a little girl she had to live in the town.'

'Did she now?' Matt absorbed this information, wondering how true it was. He hesitated, loath to pump the child, but compelled to do so anyway, 'Did she tell you anything else?'

'Just that she never had a dog when she was little,' said Rosie thoughtfully. 'I'll ask her where she came from, if you like.'

'No.' Matt spoke sharply and the little girl's jaw quivered in response.

'All right,' she said, getting down from the bed. 'I won't say anything. But I think you're really—really mean.'

'Ah, Rosie—' Matt rolled to the side of the bed and grabbed his daughter's arm before she could get away. 'Honey, try to understand. You're very precious. How can I leave you with someone I hardly know?'

'You didn't know any of the other girls who came for the job,' replied Rosie tremulously, and Matt groaned.

'Baby, they came from an agency.'

'So?'

'So—' He pulled her towards the bed and swung his feet to the floor. Then, placing a hand on either side of her small waist, he gave her a gentle shake. 'Try to understand, sweetheart. I don't like disappointing you, but—'

'Then don't,' pleaded Rosie, seizing the opportunity. 'Give Sara a chance, please! I promise I'll be good. I won't play her up like I used to with Hester.'

'It's not you I'm worried about,' muttered Matt, but he was hesitating. His common sense was telling him to stick to his guns, to ignore the emotional demands his daughter was making on him, but his instincts were telling him something else.

All right, he knew nothing about Sara, but he'd bet his last cent that, whatever she was running away from, she was not a bad person. There was something innately honest about her, an integrity that was at odds with all he knew and suspected about her.

'Daddy...'

Rosie's wheedling voice made his decision for him. 'All

right,' he said, praying he wouldn't have cause to regret the impulse. 'We'll give her a few days' trial—'

'Hurray!' Rosie was excited.

'—but I'm making no promises beyond the weekend, right?'

'All right.' Rosie clasped her hands together. 'Can I go and ask her? Can I? Can I? I'm sure when she knows that you want her to stay she'll change her mind—'

'Hold on.' Matt held on to the little girl when she would have darted towards the door. 'What do you mean, you're sure she'll change her mind? What have you been saying to her, Rosie? Come on. I want to know.'

Rosie heaved a heavy sigh. 'Nothing much,' she mumbled, the sulkiness returning to her expression. 'I just said I wished she could stay, that's all.' She gave a jerky shrug. 'If you want to know, she said she couldn't.' And then, as her father gave her a stunned look, she added, 'But I know she wanted to, Daddy. Only she thought you didn't want her here.'

Matt stared. 'Did she say that?'

'No.' Rosie spoke crossly. 'I've told you what she said.'

'Are you sure?'

'Yes.' Rosie was indignant. 'Don't you believe me?'

Matt pulled a wry face. 'Do I have a choice?'

'So?' Rosie pulled her lower lip between her teeth. 'Can I go and ask her?'

Matt glanced at the clock on the cabinet beside the bed. 'Not yet,' he said heavily, already regretting his generosity. 'It's barely seven o'clock. We'll discuss it some more at breakfast.'

He let the little girl go, but now Rosie hesitated. 'You won't put her off, will you, Daddy?' she persisted. 'I mean, you will let her know that we—that we'd *both* like her to stay?'

Matt stifled an oath. 'Don't push your luck, Rosie,' he said, without making any promises. 'Go get your wash, and clean your teeth. As I say, we'll talk about this later. If that's not good enough for you we'd better forget the whole thing.'

Rosie's chin wobbled again, but she managed to control it. 'All right, Daddy,' she said huskily, and with a tearful smile she made good her escape before he changed his mind again.

*   *   *

Mrs Webb had arrived by the time Matt came downstairs.

The housekeeper, who was in her middle fifties, had worked at Seadrift for as long as Matt had owned the house, and there was usually an easy familiarity between them that wasn't much in evidence this morning.

However, there was a welcome pot of coffee simmering on the hob and, after giving her his usual greeting, Matt went to help himself to a cup. He hoped the caffeine would kick-start his brain, which seemed to have blanked during his conversation with Rosie. Why, in God's name, had he given in to her? What had possessed him to agree to asking Sara to stay?

'I understand you've got a new nanny,' said Mrs Webb suddenly, turning from the fridge and confronting him with accusing eyes. 'You didn't tell me you were interviewing anyone yesterday.'

Matt expelled a disbelieving breath. 'Who told you we had a new nanny?' he demanded, but he already knew. Gloria Armstrong would have lost no time in ringing his housekeeper to hear all the lurid details. He only hoped Mrs Webb hadn't said anything to expose the lie.

He was wrong, however. 'Rosie, actually,' she replied huffily, peeling the plastic wrap from a packet of bacon. 'She couldn't wait to tell me the woman had stayed the night.'

Matt gave an inward groan. 'Well—it's not settled yet,' he said lamely, silently berating his daughter for her big mouth. 'And—and the reason I didn't tell you I was interviewing anyone yesterday was because I didn't have any plans to do so.'

'Oh, right.' Mrs Webb regarded him sceptically. 'So she just turned up out of the blue?' She grimaced. 'How convenient.'

Matt's patience grew taut. 'Actually, it wasn't convenient at all,' he declared tersely. 'And, as I say, I'm not absolutely sure I'm going to employ her.'

'So where did she come from? The agency?'

'No.' Matt blew out a breath. 'As a matter of fact, her car broke down at the bottom of the road. Didn't you see it as you came by?'

Mrs Webb looked surprised. 'So that's *her* car. I assumed

some kids had stolen it and abandoned it when it ran out of petrol.'

'No.' But Matt was determined not to be drawn into telling the housekeeper the whole story. Not yet, anyway. 'She—she came to the house, wanting to use the phone, and when she discovered I was looking for a nanny she offered herself for the job.' He paused, and then went on doggedly, 'She used to be a primary school teacher.'

'Really?'

'Yes, really.' Matt wondered why it sounded so much more convincing the second time around. 'Now, where is Rosie? I want to speak to her.'

'Oh, I think she went upstairs again,' said Mrs Webb, obviously mollified by his explanation. 'She said something about waking—Sara, is it?'

Dammit! Matt suppressed another oath. What in hell's name did Rosie think she was up to? He'd told her he'd discuss Sara's employment at breakfast. He just hoped she hadn't jumped the gun.

Snatching up the morning newspaper that Mrs Webb always brought for him, he stalked out of the kitchen and into the library. Seating himself in the hide-covered chair beside the desk which he used for his research, he took another long swig of his coffee and then turned to stare broodingly out of the windows.

Beyond the cliffs, the sun had already spread its bounty across the dark blue waters of the bay. Whereas the day before it had been cloudy, this morning the sky was high and clear. Seagulls soared effortlessly on the thermals, their haunting cries mingling with the muted roar of the surf. In an ideal world he shouldn't have a care in the world, beyond the problems facing the protagonist in his current manuscript. Indeed, after taking Rosie to school he'd intended to spend the whole day finalising the book's denouement. Instead he had to deal with a situation that he very much suspected was far more complex than his uninvited guest was letting on.

Scowling, he flipped open the newspaper that he'd dropped on the desk. The latest images from a middle-eastern war he felt he had no part of dominated the front page. There'd been a derailment in southeast London, a well-known politician had been discovered in compromising circumstances, and someone who'd won the lottery six months ago was now broke again.

So what's new? thought Matt cynically, swallowing another mouthful of coffee. Why did journalists feel the need to fill their columns with negative news items? he wondered. Was it because stories about other people's problems, particularly the rich and famous, made the average reader feel better about their own lives?

Probably, he decided, flicking the pages. There was nothing like learning about someone else's misfortunes to make some people feel good.

He heard Rosie come scampering down the stairs and remembered he had his own problems to deal with. He'd half risen from his chair to go after her when a small picture towards the bottom of page four caught his eye. Sinking back into his seat, he stared at it disbelievingly. It was a picture of Sara, he saw incredulously. Only her name wasn't Sara; it was Victoria. Victoria Bradbury, actually. The wife of the entrepreneur Max Bradbury, and she was missing.

Victoria, he thought, acknowledging the connotation. Miss *Victor* hadn't wanted to stray too far from the truth. But no wonder she didn't want to tell him who she was. Although Matt had only heard Max Bradbury's name in passing, she didn't know that.

He read the article through, his brows drawing together as he assessed its content. According to the writer, Victoria Bradbury had disappeared two nights ago, and both her husband and her mother were frantic with worry. Mr Bradbury had apparently had a fall the same evening, which was why his wife's disappearance hadn't been noted until the following morning.

Luckily Mr Bradbury had been able to crawl to a phone and summon assistance before losing consciousness. His brother, the actor Hugo Bradbury, had said it was most unlike Victoria to leave the apartment without informing her husband where she was going. Fears were being expressed that she might have been kidnapped. Mr Bradbury had been detained in hospital over-

night for tests, but had discharged himself the following morning to conduct the search for his wife personally. Max Bradbury
was an extremely wealthy man and he intended to use all means
at his disposal to find her.

The article ended with an appeal that anyone who might have
seen Mrs Bradbury or knew of her whereabouts should contact
the police and a London number was supplied.

Matt blew out a breath, slumping back in his chair and staring
incredulously out of the window. Then, snatching up the newspaper again, he examined Sara's—*Victoria's*—picture more
closely. It had to be her. He would swear it.

It was a more sophisticated Victoria than he was used to
seeing, of course. For one thing she wasn't wearing her hair in
a plait. Instead, it was coiled into a knot on top of her head.
The carefully coaxed strands that framed her face and curved
so confidingly beneath her jawline were familiar, and the wide-
spaced eyes, the high cheekbones, the generous, yet curiously
vulnerable mouth were unmistakable. Unless she had an iden-
tical twin, he was looking at a picture of the woman who had
spent last night in his spare room. Dammit, what was she playing at?

Anger gripped him. It infuriated him that he'd been taken in
by her air of vulnerability. Hell, he'd felt sorry for her. He
hadn't believed her story, of course, and that was one thing in
his favour, but he had felt a sense of responsibility for her which
he realised now had been totally misplaced. She must have been
laughing at him all along.

Max Bradbury's wife. He scowled. He wondered how long
they'd been married. To his knowledge Bradbury was at least
fifty, which must make him more than twenty years older than
his wife. So what had gone wrong? Had she become bored with
the old man? Hadn't he been giving her enough attention? Was
this escapade intended to remind him how lucky he was to have
such a young and attractive wife?

And, if so, what was the idea of asking for a job? Of pretending that she'd once been a primary school teacher. For
God's sake, a man like Max Bradbury wouldn't have married

a schoolteacher. No, she had to have been some kind of party girl or socialite. How else could she have met a man like him?

'Breakfast's ready, Daddy.'

Rosie's voice calling his name alerted him to the fact that it wasn't only his feelings Victoria Bradbury had insulted. It was his daughter's, too, and he dreaded having to tell the little girl that 'Sara' wouldn't be staying.

But he couldn't do that now. Before he made any decisions he might later regret he was going to have a frank discussion with his house guest and find out where the hell she got off, making a fool of him and his daughter. And after that he was going to ring the number they'd given in the newspaper. It would give him great satisfaction to send Victoria Bradbury back where she belonged.

Or would it?

His scowl deepened, and he quickly folded the newspaper and stuffed it into one of the drawers of the desk just as Rosie appeared in the doorway.

'Are you coming, Daddy?' she exclaimed, though there was a tentative note in her voice, and he remembered what he'd been going to do before the article in the newspaper had distracted him. 'Mrs Webb says breakfast is ready.'

'Is—Sara—up?' he asked, guessing his daughter would assume he was angry with her for disobeying him, and she gave a nervous shrug.

'She's in the dining room,' she said. And then added quickly, 'I haven't told her anything about what we were talking about, Daddy. Honestly. I just wanted to—to—'

'To see if she'd slept all right?' suggested Matt, helping her out, and Rosie gave a relieved nod.

'That's right,' she said. 'Are you coming?'

'I'm coming.' Matt paused only long enough to swallow the last dregs of coffee in his mug. 'You lead the way.'

Mrs Webb had laid the table in the dining room and was fussing about with a jug of freshly squeezed orange juice and a rack of toast. Matt guessed she was curious about their guest, too, and she was asking her what had gone wrong with her car when he entered the room.

Although she was answering the housekeeper's question at the time, Matt noticed the way Sara-Victoria's eyes darted to his face when he appeared. If he wasn't mistaken, there was a definite trace of trepidation in her gaze, and he wondered if she'd realised that her disappearance might have warranted media attention.

'Good morning,' he said, deliberately adopting an upbeat tone, and he saw the relieved hint of colour that entered her pale cheeks at his words.

She was wearing her own clothes again this morning, and Matt's eyes were irresistibly drawn to the taut breasts pushing at the semi-transparent fabric of her dress. Its shades of blue and green matched the luminescence of her eyes, which he was aware were watching him with wary intensity. Slim arms were wrapped protectively about her midriff, and he wondered if she realised what a giveaway that was.

'Um—good morning,' she responded at last, and Matt despised the sudden surge of blood that her husky voice caused to rush to his groin. All of a sudden he was remembering the sexual fantasies he'd been having about her earlier, and even the fact that he now knew she was another man's wife didn't make them any the easier to dismiss.

'Sit here, Daddy.'

Rosie pulled him to the seat beside hers, and Matt strove to act naturally. Hell, he thought, he was behaving as if he'd never been with a woman before. What was there about Victoria Bradbury that struck such a chord in his subconscious? What was there about her wary face that inspired thoughts of naked bodies and sweat-soaked sheets?

'Did you sleep well?' he asked at length, realising that, however much he might want to, he couldn't broach the subject of her identity while Rosie and Mrs Webb were present. In fact, he wouldn't be able to speak to her at all until Rosie had been delivered to school, and that might prove something of a problem. After all, he'd promised his daughter to discuss the subject of Sara's employment at breakfast.

'Very well,' she replied politely, evidently taking her cue from him, though he doubted she was being entirely honest.

Although she'd done her best to disguise them, there were still dark rings around her eyes, and, knowing what he knew now, he wasn't really surprised. 'It's so peaceful here.'

'Sara likes the seaside, Daddy,' put in Rosie eagerly, evidently hoping to prompt him into saying something positive, but it was Mrs Webb who spoke next.

'You're not from around here, are you, Miss Victor?' she observed, setting a bowl of cornflakes in front of Rosie. 'If I'm not mistaken, that's a southern accent.'

Matt saw the way the younger woman stiffened at these words, but she managed to produce a tight smile. 'I—yes. You're right. I'm from London,' she admitted, with obvious reluctance. Then, changing the subject, 'Just toast for me, please.'

'Are you sure?'

Mrs Webb was persistent and, taking pity on his guest, Matt intervened. 'I think we're all set here,' he said, regarding his own plate of bacon and eggs without enthusiasm. 'If we need anything else I'll come and find you. Okay?'

'Well—if you say so.' Mrs Webb wasn't giving up without a struggle. 'Couldn't I tempt you with an omelette, Miss Victor?'

Matt felt Sara's eyes dart to his again, and he guessed she was remembering the lunch he had made her the previous day. 'Toast is fine,' she insisted, and the housekeeper had to accept defeat.

'I'll leave you, then,' she said, giving Matt a speaking look. 'Remember, Rosie's got to leave for school in less than twenty minutes.'

'I haven't forgotten,' said Matt drily. 'Thank you.'

Mrs Webb pursed her lips and left the room, and as soon as the door had banged behind her Rosie made a face. 'She's cross because Daddy didn't ask her to sit with us and have her coffee,' she confided, with a giggle. 'We usually have breakfast in the kitchen, you see.'

'Oh.'

Sara looked to Matt for confirmation and he sighed. 'She does like to share all the village gossip,' he agreed, wishing

Rosie wasn't quite so candid. He pushed the toast rack towards Sara. 'Help yourself.'

'Thanks.'

She took a slice of toast and spread it thinly with butter, but once again Matt noticed that she barely touched it. At this rate she'd be just skin and bone in no time, he mused unwillingly. But it wasn't his concern. If she'd lost her appetite, it was doubtless because she was terrified he was going to find out what a liar she was. But why was she lying? Why had she run away? What the hell was she playing at?

'You don't have to leave today, do you, Sara?' Rosie asked now, nudging her father's ankle with her foot. And, although he gave her a warning look, she went on bravely, 'Sara could stay—' she faltered '—stay until tomorrow, couldn't she?'

'I don't think so,' Sara began, and although Matt was tempted to let her leave and be done with it, he saw his daughter's face and relented.

'Yes, stay,' he said flatly, deciding that she deserved the chance to explain why she'd been lying. And this way he could ensure that she'd still be here when he got back from taking Rosie to school. 'At least until tomorrow.'

He could see her indecision. She was probably weighing the advantages of staying here, where she believed no one knew who she was, against moving on and risking inevitable exposure. He was also aware that his own feelings were just as ambivalent. Dammit, he didn't owe her a thing, he told himself savagely. Yet he couldn't deny he felt sorry for her.

And how sensible was that?

CHAPTER SIX

SARA went back to her room after Matt had left to take Rosie to school. She wanted to avoid giving Mrs Webb the chance to ask any more questions. She was unpleasantly surprised to find that the bed she'd slept in had already been made.

Which meant the housekeeper must have accomplished this task while they were downstairs having breakfast. She didn't for one minute think that Matt would have made her bed, and she wondered uneasily what the woman had thought of the fact that she didn't have any luggage.

For she had no doubt that Mrs Webb would have noticed. She might not have actually interfered with any of her belongings, but in the course of her work she was bound to have opened the bathroom door and seen that there was no toothbrush on the shelf.

Closing the door behind her, Sara leaned heavily back against the panels. Why had she agreed to stay on for another day? Why, when she'd realised what a gossip Mrs Webb was, hadn't she made her excuses and left? Because her car was still not fixed, she reminded herself impatiently. Perhaps she should contact the rental agency, which was a countrywide operation after all, and ask them to supply her with a new car?

But, no. That would be foolish, she realised at once. At the moment all anyone knew was that she'd left the apartment. She'd deliberately not taken her own car because registration plates were so easy to trace. In time they might get around to checking with the rental agencies, but by then she intended to have abandoned the car in favour of some other form of transport.

The trouble was, she needed money. She hadn't thought of that when she'd left London, and although she'd used her credit card to hire the car she hadn't considered using a cash machine until she'd been forced to stop for petrol. Then she'd realised

that to do so would alert the authorities to her current whereabouts and she'd used most of her cash for the fill-up.

Working for Matt Seton would have solved all her problems,
she thought regretfully. But she should have known that any
legitimate employer would want the kind of personal details that
she couldn't supply. Not to mention references, she remembered
wearily. And who could blame him for that?

She knew the most sensible thing would be to leave now,
before she said or did something to betray herself. Before she
got in too deep, she acknowledged tensely. Last night there'd
been times when she'd almost forgotten the events that had
brought her here, when she'd begun to relax and enjoy herself.
Did that make her a bad person? she wondered. Was the fact
that for the first time in years she'd been able to be herself
without fear of retribution a cause for self-disgust?

Max would have thought so. Max would have been incensed
at her behaviour. He didn't like children and he'd have accused
her of using Rosie to get to Matt. He'd have said that allowing
the little girl to paint her nails had just been a way of attracting
Matt's attention. Max had been insanely jealous, as she knew
to her cost, and he'd have turned an innocent game into something ugly.

Yet had it been so innocent? she fretted uneasily. Perhaps
she was the provocative little tease that Max had always accused
her of being. It was certainly true that she'd been acutely aware
of Matt Seton ever since he'd emerged from his Range Rover
the day before. In spite of her apprehension she'd recognised
him at once for what he was: a disturbingly attractive man who
she had soon realised was nothing like Max.

Thank God!

She didn't know how she had been so sure of that. It wasn't
as if she was a terrifically good judge of character. She'd married Max Bradbury, hadn't she? Her lips twisted. She'd thought
he was a good man. Because he was so much older than she
was, she'd trusted him. She'd actually believed that his promise
to take her away from what he'd convinced her was a boring
existence had been inspired by love and not by an unnatural

desire for possession. Instead, he'd turned her life into a nightmare, and even now he was still controlling her from the grave.

She shuddered. What was she doing, thinking about Matt Seton when it was because of her that her husband was lying cold on some mortuary slab? She could imagine how Matt would feel about her when he found out who she really was. However reluctant he'd been to offer her his hospitality up to this point would be as nothing compared to his revulsion when he discovered the truth. She was a murderess—well, she'd be convicted of manslaughter at the very least, she amended. He wouldn't want someone like her associating with his daughter.

And as for anything else... She gave a bitter smile. There were no men in a women's prison.

She moved away from the door, wincing as once again her hip reminded her of its presence. If only her car was operational, she thought fiercely. She really believed she might have made her getaway while Matt was out. It wasn't fair to involve him in her troubles. And if the police ever discovered that he'd allowed her to stay here he might be charged with harbouring a wanted criminal.

But he didn't know who she was, she assured herself, disliking that word 'criminal' again. Although she guessed it was only a matter of time before he found out. Max's death was bound to make news eventually. And, although she hadn't seen a television since she'd arrived, he was bound to have a set somewhere.

She walked restlessly to the windows. It was such a beautiful morning, she thought. She longed to get out of the house and escape her anxieties in the simple delight of feeling the wind in her hair and the sun on her face. Who knew how much longer she'd be free to enjoy such simple pleasures? Oughtn't she to make the most of it while she had the chance?

Despite being reluctant to meet Mrs Webb again, she opened her door and stepped out onto the landing. A railed gallery overlooked the main entrance and she saw to her relief that there was no sign of the housekeeper in the hall below.

Matt hadn't used this door the day before, but, having descended the stairs on tiptoe, Sara prayed it wouldn't present any problems now. She was unutterably relieved when the key turned and the handle yielded to her touch. Stepping outside, into the sunshine, she took a deep breath of the salt-laden air.

She heard the dogs barking as she walked across the forecourt. Their hearing was obviously sharper than Mrs Webb's, and Sara hoped the housekeeper would be too busy quieting them to notice her slipping out of the gates.

She wanted to go down to the beach if she could, but, remembering the steepness of the path they'd used the afternoon before, she guessed that was the only means of access. It meant circling the house again, but luckily the track beyond the gates led onto the cliffs without having to re-enter the property.

All the same, she was glad when she started down the path and the cliff face hid her descent from view. It wasn't that she was afraid of being seen, she assured herself. She wasn't a prisoner yet, for heaven's sake. She just needed a little time alone to think about what she was going to do next.

She must have walked at least a quarter of a mile along the beach when she heard someone calling her name.

She had been enjoying the unaccustomed freedom. The breeze was warmer today, and she could smell the sea. The damp sand had been totally untouched when she'd started along the shoreline, and she knew her footprints would soon be washed away by the incoming tide.

Hearing her name, however, she expelled a sigh and stopped. She didn't even have to turn to know who it was. Only Matt Seton knew she was staying here; only he was likely to come after her.

Stifling her resentment, she turned. As if he couldn't have allowed her to finish her walk in peace, she was thinking half irritably. For heaven's sake, he wasn't her keeper.

The sight that met her startled eyes caused her to quickly revise her opinion, however. Matt was still some distance away, but between them lapped a rapidly expanding stretch of water that successfully trapped her between the incoming tide and the cliffs. Fairly deep water, too, she saw, trying not to panic. It had already covered the rocks that formed a sort of breakwater at the foot of the headland.

As she watched, she saw Matt break into a run, splashing into the water that divided them with grim determination. 'Stay where you are,' he yelled, wading towards her, and Sara stood there, dry-mouthed, as he closed the space between them. The water came up to his thighs, she saw, soaking his jeans and plastering them to the powerful muscles of his legs. Despite the sunshine, she felt sure the water must be icy. It was far too early in the day for the sun to have gained any strength.

She watched his approach anxiously, wondering what she would have done if he hadn't appeared. She could keep herself afloat, but she wasn't a strong swimmer. If Max were here, he'd tell her how stupid she was.

Matt reached her without too much difficulty and she looked up at him with apologetic eyes. 'I should have told Mrs Webb where I was going, shouldn't I?' she began, before he could say a word. 'I'm sorry. I just wanted a walk. I had no idea—'

Her voice trailed away and Matt expelled a resigned sigh. 'Yeah, well, let's get you back before we start the inquest, shall we?' he suggested flatly. 'Here: there's no point in both of us getting soaked to the skin. I'll carry you.'

'Oh, that's not necess—' she started, but Matt wasn't listening to her. Before she knew what was happening, he'd swung her up into his arms. But she couldn't prevent the groan of agony that escaped her lips when his thoughtless handling brought her bruised hip into sharp contact with his pelvis. The pain was sharper than ever and it was difficult to get her breath.

Matt was instantly aware of her reaction. 'Did I hurt you?' he asked, frowning, and she guessed he'd seen the way the colour had drained out of her face.

'I—it's nothing,' she assured him quickly, not wanting to arouse his curiosity. 'You gave me a shock. I could have walked, you know.'

Matt looked as if that was open to discussion. But once again the precariousness of their situation forced him to put his own feelings on hold. 'Hang on,' was all he permitted himself, before plunging back into the water, heading for the dry sand further along the beach.

She put her arms around his neck, unafraid that they wouldn't

make it. She trusted Matt implicitly, she realised, more aware
of the strength of his arms supporting her than the chilly waters
of the North Sea surging below. And, although every movement
he made caused the fabric of her dress to chafe her sore skin,
she bore it gratefully. The warmth of his body soothed her like
nothing else she could remember.

Which was crazy, she chided herself impatiently, trying not
to notice the length of his eyelashes or the darkening line of
stubble on his jaw. Such a strong jawline, she mused, aware of
him with every cell in her being. This close, she could see every
pore and bristle, was only inches away from the sensual curve
of his mouth.

His breath fanned her temple, warm and only slightly fla-
voured with the strong black coffee he'd drunk at breakfast.
She could smell the soap he used, smell his sweat. And was
helplessly aware of her own reactions to him.

She was instantly ashamed. She had no right to be speculating on what it would be like to be in his arms because he
wanted her there. It was useless to wonder how she'd feel if he
touched her, touched her intimately. But, if he allowed her slim
frame to slide against him, would she find he was aroused?

She sucked in her breath. This had to stop, she told herself
fiercely. She'd never had thoughts like this before. She'd certainly never considered herself a sexual woman. The only man
she'd ever known intimately was Max.

Her husband's name acted like a douche of cold water. She
shivered violently and Matt, misunderstanding, said sharply,
'Are you getting wet?'

'No.'

Her response was sharper than it might have been because
of the way she was feeling, and Matt arched an ironic brow.
'Well, we're nearly there,' he said, nodding towards the dry
sand directly ahead of them. 'I should have warned you about
the tides around here. They can be dangerous.'

Sara shook her head. 'It wasn't your fault,' she said, turning
to see the cliff path just a few yards away. 'You can put me
down now.'

'Perhaps I don't want to,' remarked Matt, stepping out of the water onto the patch of sand that was still uncovered by the tide. He looked down into her startled face and she was uneasily aware of how emotionally vulnerable she was. 'I think you and I need to have a little talk, Mrs Bradbury.' He allowed her name to register with her. 'Don't you?'

Sara could scarcely breathe. 'How do you know who I am?' she asked, not bothering to try and deny it, and Matt hesitated only a moment before setting her on her feet.

'How do you think?' he asked, stepping away from her. 'I saw your picture in a newspaper, of course.' He paused, looking back at her. 'Look, do you mind if we continue this after I've got out of these wet clothes?'

Sara's mouth felt so dry she doubted her ability to speak. But she had to say something in her own defence. Swallowing, she whispered, 'It—it was an accident, you know. It wasn't my fault.' She drew a breath. 'I—I didn't mean to—'

'Deceive me?' Matt finished the sentence he thought she'd started in a dry, cynical voice. 'Yeah, right.' He glanced towards the path again. 'Well, like I say, I'd prefer to have this conversation when I'm not in danger of freezing my butt, okay?'

He attempted to pull the soaked jeans away from his legs, but only succeeded in drawing Sara's eyes to the way the denim was drawn taut over the swell of his sex. He intercepted her stare and gave a wry grimace. 'Sorry if I'm embarrassing you, Mrs Bradbury,' he added mockingly. 'I guess I'm not as cold as I thought.'

Sara's face flamed. 'You're not embarrassing me,' she exclaimed, even though her face was bright red. Now she looked anywhere but at his crotch. 'Would you prefer me to go first?'

Matt's lips twisted. 'Yes, I'd prefer you to go first,' he mimicked her prim tone. 'And when we get back to the house you're going to let Mrs Webb take a look at that hip. I know it's hurting you, and the old lady used to be a nursing auxiliary until she had a family and had to give it up.'

Sara pressed her lips together. This wasn't the time to argue with him, as he'd said, but she hoped he didn't think the fact that he'd discovered who she was gave him the right to order her about. She had no intention of letting Mrs Webb or anyone else examine her. If she was arrested— She licked her dry lips. Well, she'd face that problem when she came to it. Until then…

It was harder climbing the cliff path today than it had been the day before. She assumed fear—and the prospect of imminent exposure to the authorities—had stiffened her muscles, and it was difficult putting one foot in front of the other.

On top of that, her mind was buzzing with thoughts of what Matt intended to do with her. Had he already called the police? Or was he prepared to listen to her side of the story before turning her in? Although she knew there was no chance of her getting away, she couldn't help considering and discarding every option open to her.

Reaching the house, she had only Mrs Webb's ire to contend with, however. The housekeeper clicked her tongue when she saw Matt's wet clothes and said, 'Go and get into a hot shower before you catch your death.' Then she turned on Sara. 'You should have told me you were going out,' she exclaimed shortly. 'I would have warned you about the tides.'

'I know.'

Sara was contrite, but Matt chose to intervene. 'Give her a break,' he said, heading for the hall. 'She's had a shock. And, as far as getting wet is concerned, it is the middle of June, not November.'

'And that water's warm, is it?' Mrs Webb enquired, with some sarcasm, and he sighed.

'Warm enough,' he said, not to be outdone. 'Right. I'll see you in about fifteen minutes.'

Sara knew this remark was addressed to her, but she had no intention of staying in the kitchen until he returned. It was to avoid the housekeeper's questions that she'd sneaked out in the first place, and although she was fairly sure Matt hadn't told Mrs Webb who she was, she wasn't prepared to take that chance.

She waited until Matt had disappeared upstairs before saying casually, 'I'll be in my room, if anyone wants me.'

'Why don't you stay here?' The housekeeper sounded put out. 'Unless I'm not good enough for you, that is.'

Sara blew out a breath. 'I need to use the bathroom,' she said evenly. 'It has nothing to do with your company, I can assure you.'

Mrs Webb regarded her grudgingly. 'Matt says you're staying until tomorrow,' she remarked conversationally. 'Have you—er—have you known him long?'

Sara blinked. 'Matt?' She shook her head 'I only met him yesterday. I thought you knew.'

'I know what he said,' declared the housekeeper narrowly, looking sceptical. 'But he seems awfully concerned about someone he only met twenty-four hours ago.'

Sara wished she'd left when Matt had. Whatever she felt about it, Mrs Webb was determined to get her pound of flesh. 'I meant it,' she said, 'we barely know one another.'

But she couldn't help wondering what the housekeeper would say if she was honest. She and Matt might only have known one another for a short time, but their relationship couldn't be judged in terms of hours and minutes. Despite the shortness of their association, he probably knew her more intimately than anyone else.

Mrs Webb shrugged and returned to the casserole she'd been preparing before they came in, and Sara took the opportunity to get away. Favouring her uninjured leg, she left the kitchen, going as swiftly as she could up the stairs and along the gallery to her room.

It was amazing how quickly this room had become her refuge, she thought, sinking down onto the bed. It wasn't her room, and it certainly wasn't anything like the room she'd shared with Max. But it was bright and cheerful, and she felt at home there.

Which she had never done in the luxurious duplex apartment she shared with her husband. Situated in a fashionable part of the city, it had been decorated and furnished by a firm of interior designers that Max thought highly of. She'd had no say in any of it. The apartment was expensive and soulless, and she hated everything about it.

Or perhaps she'd simply hated the life she'd lived there, she acknowledged bitterly. Like his Rolex watch, his Armani suits

and his Bentley, she had been just another of Max's possessions. The only difference had been that he had treated his
watch, his clothes and his car rather better than his wife.

Her hip throbbed, reminding her that she ought to check and
see that it hadn't started bleeding. The skin had been seriously
scrubbed in places, and it wouldn't be the first time that she'd
had to repair the damage. But this time she didn't have a convenient wardrobe of clothes to change into, and she could imagine Matt's reaction if he saw blood on her dress.

Lifting the hem of her skirt, she examined the injury, noticing
that the skin was badly inflamed. But that was because of the
way Matt had carried her, and she could hardly blame him for
trying to save her life.

Nevertheless, there was a faint trace of blood oozing from
the point of her hip and she clicked her tongue in frustration.
Now what was she going to do? She didn't carry any adhesive
plasters in her haversack. Perhaps she'd find some in the bathroom cabinet. It was the kind of thing people did keep in case
of emergency.

Holding her skirt to her waist, she got up from the bed and
limped into the bathroom. Then, clutching her dress in one
hand, she reached up to the cabinet with the other.

'Sara?'

It was Matt's voice and she panicked. He mustn't see her
like this. All right, so he probably knew about Max's accident,
but there was no need for him to witness her humiliation. If he
chose to call the police she couldn't stop him. But she could
hold onto her dignity until then.

Pushing the bathroom door to with her uninjured hip, she
called weakly, 'What do you want?'

'Can I come in?'

Sara breathed a little more easily. She'd thought at first that
he was in. 'Why?' she asked, suddenly remembering what he'd
said about Mrs Webb. 'I don't need any assistance.'

'I'm not offering any,' he replied, his voice louder now. 'I've
brought you a gift.'

A gift!

Sara blinked. What kind of gift could he have brought her?

Some more of his old clothes? Or perhaps he wanted to show her the newspaper where he'd read about her? That seemed infinitely more likely.

'I—just leave it on the bed,' she called, deciding there was no point in expecting him to go away without achieving his objective. 'I'll be out in a minute.'

There was silence for a moment, and then she heard Matt's voice just outside the bathroom door. 'What are you doing?' he exclaimed. 'Is your hip all right?'

Sara trembled. 'It's fine,' she insisted. 'What do people usually do in the bathroom?' She closed the door of the cabinet, just in case he came to investigate, but that was a mistake. She had evidently dislodged the items inside and a tube of hair gel came clattering down into the basin in front of her.

'What the—?' Without more ado, the bathroom door was forced open, and Matt stood on the threshold staring at her with bleak horrified eyes. 'For God's sake,' he exclaimed, staring at her injury. 'Did I do that?'

'As if.' Sara managed the contemptuous rejoinder with amazing composure. But then, realising that her lacy briefs left very little to his imagination, she allowed her skirt to fall and sagged against the basin. 'I had a fall before I came away.'

Matt gave a disbelieving snort. 'You do a lot of falling in your house, don't you?'

'What do you mean?' Sara stared at him with confused eyes.

'Your husband,' he stated flatly, his eyes still fixed on the spot her skirt had now hidden from his gaze. 'He fell, too. What a coincidence!'

Sara's shoulders slumped. 'You don't know anything about it.'

'No.' Matt agreed. 'But I'm willing to listen if you want to tell me. I'm not jumping to conclusions here, but a simple fall wouldn't have caused that mess.'

'It did.' Sara was desperate. 'It was an accident. I didn't mean it to happen. And that's the truth.'

Matt's brows drew together. 'Hey, I'm not accusing you of anything,' he protested. His eyes darkened. 'I'd guess it had something to do with your running away, right?'

'If you say so.' Sara spoke wearily. 'So what now? Are you going to turn me in?'

Matt eyes sought hers. 'Turn you in?' he echoed blankly. 'You talk as if you're a criminal. The last I heard, running away isn't a capital offence.'

'Running away?' She repeated his words barely audibly. 'But you said you knew about—about Max having a fall.'

'So?'

'So—so what did it say about how they found him? Did it tell you the way he—he died?'

'He's not dead!' Matt spoke harshly now. He stared at her. 'Why would you think he was?' He shook his head. 'He apparently had the presence of mind to call the emergency services before he passed out. He spent the night in hospital and discharged himself yesterday morning. That's when you were reported missing. According to the article I read, your husband's afraid you might have been kidnapped.'

CHAPTER SEVEN

MATT wouldn't have believed Sara could get any paler, but she did. Every scrap of colour drained out of her face, leaving her unnaturally pallid. The circles around her eyes stood out in sharp relief and her mouth worked in silent consternation.

'You're—you're lying,' she got out at last, and he wondered why, if she'd believed her husband was dead, the news that he wasn't should have such a shattering effect.

'Why would I lie?' he reasoned, becoming anxious in spite of himself. 'Sara—'

'Max calls me Victoria,' she said dully. 'You must know that.' Then she slid to the floor in a dead faint.

It was the second time he'd had to pick her unconscious body off the floor. Not that she weighed much. She felt wholly insubstantial in his arms. How long was it since she'd eaten a decent meal? he wondered. In the last twenty-four hours she'd only picked at her food, and he suspected her weakness was due in part to hunger.

So, why? Why had she been starving herself? Why had she run away? And how had she sustained such an ugly bruise on her hip? As Matt carried her into the bedroom and laid her on the bed his mind buzzed with a jumble of questions. The most obvious explanation was fear. But what was she afraid of?

He straightened and stood looking down at her. He wished he could believe she was a spoiled wife who had grown bored with her pampered existence and decided to give her husband a wake-up call. Could she really have been that self-indulgent? Somehow he didn't buy it.

Her eyelids were fluttering and, realising that in a short time she was going to be wide awake and denying everything he was thinking, Matt came to an abrupt decision. Hoping she wouldn't object too much, he took the hem of her skirt and drew it up to her waist.

He was shocked again by the sight of the ugly lesions on her hip, but he knew he didn't have time to examine them more closely right now. Instead, he slipped his arm beneath her and eased her dress out of the way.

She began to protest now as consciousness returned, trying to push his hands away without any success. Matt wasn't listening to her. Horror had replaced his concern and he sank down onto the bed beside her in speechless disbelief.

There was barely an inch of her torso that didn't bear the scars of injuries old and new. Some bruises were obviously more recent than others, the colours ranging from stark black and blue to a jaundiced yellow or brown. She'd been beaten, and beaten badly, and Matt wanted to take the man who'd done this to her and wring his cowardly neck.

His hands trembled as he eased the dress away. Sara seemed to realise there was no point in trying to stop him. It was too late; too late for both of them. Matt closed his eyes for a moment against the murderous rage that was demanding revenge.

'Your husband did this to you?' he asked at last, when he had himself in control again, and she shrugged.

'Does it matter?' She sighed. His hands lingered at her waist. 'I think you'd better let me get up.'

'And I think you ought to have that hip treated,' said Matt flatly. 'From what I've seen, it needs medical attention.'

Her response was urgent. 'I don't need a doctor,' she exclaimed fiercely, and he didn't think this was the time to tell her that that was what he had been before he'd become a writer.

He expelled an unsteady breath, hoping she wouldn't mistake his concern for something less commendable. 'I've got some first aid stuff in my bathroom. I suggest you let me deal with your hip if you don't want me to involve anyone else.'

'I can do it,' she protested, but once again he prevented her from getting off the bed.

'I'm sure you can. I'm sure that's what you're used to,' he muttered harshly. 'But in this instance I'd prefer it if you'd let me make sure there's no infection.'

Sara made a weary sound. 'There is no infection,' she insisted. 'It's just bleeding a bit, that's all.'

'So I see,' he said grimly, unable to hide his reaction. And she suddenly seemed to realise that the lower half of her body was still exposed to his gaze.

'Mr Seton—'

'Don't call me that.' He was impatient. 'It's too late for us to behave as if we're just casual acquaintances. We're not. I know it and you know it. Whether you like it not, I feel responsible for you.'

'Don't patronise me!'

'I won't if you'll do as you're told.'

Her eyes flashed with sudden spirit. 'And I'm very good at doing as I'm told,' she told him bitterly, and he groaned at his own thoughtlessness.

'Sara—'

'Shouldn't that be Victoria?' she enquired painfully. And then, as if she'd just recalled why she was lying on the bed, 'Did I pass out?'

Matt nodded. 'Like a light.' He got up. 'Stay here. Please. I'll be back in a few seconds.'

Sara looked up at him. 'You did say—Max was alive?' she ventured.

'Yes.' Matt hesitated. 'Why would you think he wasn't? What happened before you ran away?'

Sara moved her head from side to side on the pillows. 'He was so still,' she whispered, obviously thinking about it. 'I couldn't find a pulse. I was sure—' She pressed her lips together. 'Oh, God, he's going to be so mad when he finds out what I did.'

Matt felt his anger surfacing again, and determinedly forced it back. 'I'll get my gear,' he said, heading for the door. 'Just—relax, okay? I won't be long.'

She didn't answer, and he could only hope that she'd be too distracted by what he'd told her to disobey him. It wasn't just an excuse to get his hands on her again, he assured himself. She was in such a frail state she might pick up some infection without her being aware of it. He didn't want to think what the ravages of blood poisoning might do to her fragile system. He'd seen too many tragic cases in the past.

Without taking the time to check what was in the bag he kept in his bathroom, he simply snatched it out of the cupboard and charged back along the landing. Only to encounter Mrs Webb at the top of the stairs.

'Something wrong?' she asked, her sharp eyes immediately noting the medical kit. 'Do you need my help?'

Matt gave her a resigned look. 'No help needed,' he said, aware that Sara's door was ajar and that she could probably hear everything that was being said. 'Miss Victor just needs an adhesive plaster, that's all.'

'Hurt her heel, has she?' Mrs Webb arched an enquiring brow. 'I could have told her that those shoes she wears aren't suitable for around here.'

'Something like that,' Matt agreed, his nerves screaming in frustration. 'If you'll excuse me…?'

'Very formal all of a sudden, aren't we?' remarked Mrs Webb with a sniff. 'Oh, well.' To his relief she turned towards his daughter's bedroom. 'I expect I'll hear all about it from Rosie. She seems to know what's going on.'

'Nothing's going on,' said Matt, gritting his teeth, but he was talking to himself. The housekeeper was already out of earshot.

Aware of the tension in his shoulders, Matt determinedly tried to relax before going back into Sara's room. He half expected to find her locked in the bathroom, but, although she was sitting up, she was still on the bed.

'I guess you heard that,' he said, hesitating only a moment before closing the door behind him. 'My housekeeper likes to feel she's in the know.'

'Yes.' Sara's tone was dry. 'Well, I suppose it's only a matter of time before she realises who I am.'

Matt shrugged. 'We'll deal with that when we have to,' he said, sitting down beside her and opening the leather bag. 'Now, let's see: what have we got? Gauze; adhesive plasters; bandages.' His fingers hesitated over the syringe and the advantages of injection. But, dismissing the idea, he added, 'And some antiseptic ointment. Good.'

'This really isn't necessary,' she murmured, and he saw she was embarrassed all over again. She'd pulled her dress down, too, even though she was running the risk of staining it. Her dignity still meant something to her, at least.

'We have to talk,' said Matt, opening the packet of plasters and examining its contents. 'Why don't you start by telling me why you thought your husband was dead?' He paused. 'Did you try to kill him?'

'*No!*' Her denial was instantaneous, and, looking into her horrified eyes, he couldn't help but believe her. 'I wouldn't do that,' she added, with a revealing tremor in her voice. 'Max fell. Down the stairs in our apartment. I tried to find a pulse but I couldn't.' She took a breath. 'It wasn't Max who called the emergency service. It was me.'

'So why didn't you stay and speak to them?' Matt asked, hoping that by getting her to talk to him he could divert her attention. He urged her back against the pillows again, avoiding her eyes as he lifted the hem of her skirt. 'I don't understand why you ran away.'

'Don't you?' The laugh she gave was without humour. 'No, well, perhaps it is hard for you to understand how I felt. I suppose the simple answer would be to say I panicked. I was afraid no one would believe my version of events.'

Matt frowned. 'Okay,' he said evenly. 'I'll buy that. Having seen what the bastard's done to you, you've got a point.' His jaw compressed as he cleaned the abrasion on her hip with a sterile wipe. 'But for goodness' sake, Sara, why did you stay with him?'

Sara caught her breath, and he guessed her hip was stinging. 'You don't know that Max did this to me,' she argued. 'If you met him, you'd think he was a charming man. Hugo thinks so, and so does my mother. As far as she's concerned I'm an ungrateful wife.'

The area around the abrasion was clean now, and Matt stared at it for a long time, trying to contain his anger. Who the hell was Hugo? he wondered, resenting the thought that some other man might be involved. He didn't like the idea that there was someone else she cared about.

'Who is Hugo?' he asked at last, when he had himself in

control again. But the question was too personal and he felt her eyes upon him.

'Hugo is Max's brother,' she replied at last, and Matt cursed his own stupidity. He remembered now seeing the man's name in the article he'd read about her disappearance. Her lips twisted as she added, 'He's harmless.'

'But he doesn't stop his brother from beating up his wife every chance he gets,' pointed out Matt harshly, and she sighed.

'I've told you,' she said, pressing a protective hand to her midriff. 'Hugo doesn't know anything about it. He—he thinks Max and I have the ideal marriage. He's a hopeless romantic at heart.'

Hopeless? Right. Matt shook his head. But touching her was becoming the finest form of torture, and the idea that some man felt he had the right to brutalise her infuriated him anew. 'What about your father?' he demanded roughly. 'Doesn't he care?'

'My father's dead and my mother wouldn't want to believe me. She has a very comfortable lifestyle, thanks to Max,' she said unsteadily. She looked down. 'Have you finished?'

'Not nearly,' retorted Matt, his tone savage. 'Dammit, Sara, women don't have to put up with this sort of thing today. Why don't you get a divorce?'

She stiffened then. Her muscles locked, and he felt the withdrawal of a confidence he'd hardly begun to explore. 'You don't understand,' she told him tersely, and he knew if he hadn't been applying a gauze coated with antiseptic ointment to her hip at that moment she'd have scrambled off the bed and left him. She licked her lips. 'Thank you for doing this, but please don't think it gives you the right to offer me advice. I know what I'm doing—what I *have* to do. And getting a divorce isn't an option!'

'Why the hell not?'

Matt was impatient, but she just regarded him with cool guarded eyes. 'Well, your knowing who I am solves one problem,' she declared, ignoring his outburst. 'I can't stay here now.' She hesitated. 'I'll have to go back.'

'No!'

The word was torn from him. She couldn't be serious. He

tried to concentrate on the two strips of adhesive he was smoothing over the gauze. To go back to a man who clearly had no respect—let alone any love—for her. For God's sake, after what she'd told him about the circumstances of her departure he had no doubt that Max Bradbury would have reserved some particularly unpleasant punishment for embarrassing him when she got back.

His hands trembled as he completed his task but he didn't immediately release her. Although he knew she was eager to end this awkward encounter, his hands lingered on her skin. He wasn't unaware of the impropriety of his actions. He was running the risk of her accusing him of God knew what! But at that moment it wasn't important. He simply didn't want to let her go.

His eyes drifted down, over the quivering muscles of her stomach. The dusky hollow of her navel tantalised him, made him catch his breath. Below her navel the lacy briefs offered little protection, the triangular shadow that marked the apex of her legs inviting his hungry gaze.

He wanted her, he realised, even as he rejected the thought as unworthy of him. This was no fantasy; this was real, this was honest—though he doubted she'd believe his feelings had no strings attached. She'd probably find any overture he made towards her, however innocent, utterly repulsive. He wasn't arrogant enough to think she felt any attraction to him.

Yet still he prolonged the moment. And, as if becoming aware that the atmosphere between them had changed, she struggled to get up. 'Please,' she said, and although there was no fear in her eyes there was withdrawal. And a mute appeal he found hard to resist.

'You do please—me,' he told her huskily. And despite herself, he was sure, she gave a helpless little moan.

'Oh, Matt,' she whispered, her voice breaking with emotion.

And, unable to prevent himself, he bent his head and kissed her, brushing the bruised skin with his lips.

She jerked beneath his caressing touch, her hands balling into fists at her sides. He would have liked to think it was to prevent herself from touching him, but he didn't believe that. Indeed, apart from one revealing twitch, she made no move either to encourage or stop him, and Matt knew it was up to him to show some sense here.

But it was hard to be sensible. Her skin was so tender, so delicate. She tasted good, too, the light film of perspiration that had beaded her skin when he'd cleansed her hip like nectar on his tongue. Even the faint scent of the ointment was not unpleasant. It certainly wasn't enough to deter his desire. He wanted to taste every inch of her. In spite of everything, he couldn't stop.

His breath dampened her flesh. His lips burned a circle of kisses around her navel before beating a sensual path over her flat stomach. His thumbs urged the folds of the dress aside, revealing the hem of her bra. The enticing hollow between her breasts was visible to his impassioned gaze. He caught his breath. He wanted to remove her bra, to expose the rounded swell of her small breasts. He could see her nipples were already straining at the delicate lace that confined them. He longed to feel those hard peaks against his palms.

Dear God!

His own reactions to what he was doing could no longer be ignored. Between his legs his arousal throbbed with a painful insistence, and the blood was pounding in his head.

But he had to stop. With considerable effort he lifted his head and looked at her, encountering an unexpected trace of regret in her gaze. He'd expected many things: indignation; disillusionment; anger, even. What he hadn't expected was that she might actually have welcomed his lovemaking, and his brows drew together in momentary disbelief.

But her first words didn't match the fleeting expression that had now disappeared entirely. 'Are you going to let me up now?' she asked, her voice as cold as her words. 'Or are you going to demand payment for your services? Max said all men were the same in that respect.'

Matt's face flamed. Jerking back, he moved to the foot of the bed, wondering how he could have fooled himself into believing that she might want anything from him. She'd merely tolerated his lovemaking, borne his maudlin sympathies. For

God's sake, she was married to someone else. What did he expect?

But then, as if she'd instantly regretted the harshness of her words, Sara gave a despairing little moan. 'I'm sorry,' she said, pulling down her skirt and scrambling across the bed towards him. She swung her feet to the floor beside him. 'I shouldn't have said that. I didn't mean it.'

'Didn't you?' Matt wasn't prepared to put his feelings on the line again. He was already deploring the impulse that had got him into this situation. Having her forgive him for being such an idiot was no compensation at all. Getting up from the bed, he thrust his hands into the hip pockets of his jeans, swayed back on his heels with what he hoped looked like cool indifference. 'Well, that's good. I'd hate you to think I'd planned to seduce you as well.'

'I don't.' She stood up, too, and although she was considerably smaller than he was without her high heels she was still too close for comfort. 'Matt, I—I know you meant well, but—'

'Spare me the lecture,' he said, his own voice harsh in his ears. 'I've obviously embarrassed you—embarrassed us both— and I apologise.' He stepped back a pace, to put some space between them. 'I'll leave you now. You can let me know what you intend to do when—'

'No!' She caught his arm then, her cool fingers slipping almost possessively about his wrist. 'Please, Matt. Don't go away mad at me.'

Matt expelled a heavy breath, trying not to consider what she wanted now. 'I'm not mad at you,' he said, after a few moments of self-denial. Forcing himself to concentrate on the reason why he'd come to her room in the first place, he nodded towards the loveseat. 'I bought you a couple of things in Ellsmoor. You may want to change before you leave.'

Sara's lips parted. She didn't even look at the jeans and tee shirt he'd found in the mini-market. 'You want me to leave?' she asked anxiously, her hands tightening on his arm, and he stared at her with guarded eyes.

'I understood that was what you wanted,' he said, stifling the sudden urge he had to beg her to stay.

Sara swallowed. 'It's what I ought to do,' she admitted. 'My staying here—well, it could put you in an awkward position.'

'Do I look like I'm worried?' Matt's lips twisted. 'It's your decision. I'm not sending you away.'

Sara gazed up at him. 'So—I can still stay until tomorrow?'

'You can stay as long as you like,' retorted Matt roughly, taking the hand resting on his arm and raising it to his lips. His mouth grazed her knuckles before seeking the network of veins at her wrist. 'I may not approve of what you're doing, but you're safe here. I can promise you that.'

'Oh, Matt.' She brought her free hand up to his face, cupping his jaw with unsteady fingers. 'I don't know how I'm ever going to be able to thank you.'

'No thanks are necessary,' Matt told her flatly. But when he would have turned away she reached up, and pressed her lips to the corner of his mouth.

'I'd like to stay,' she whispered at last, drawing back. 'For a few days at least, if you'll let me.' She moistened her lips. 'But I'm going to have to let—let Max know that I'm all right.'

'As opposed to being at his mercy?' suggested Matt, with some bitterness, but it was a reprieve and he was grateful for it. 'Why don't you leave that to me? You write a note and I'll get it to him without running the risk of his finding out where you are.'

Her eyes widened. 'You can do that?' She trembled. 'But how?'

'You don't want to know,' replied Matt, removing her hand from his face before temptation got the better of him. Then, at the anxious look she was wearing, 'Don't worry. I won't cause any trouble. Not until I know what kind of hold he has over you, at least.'

He walked to the door, eager now to withdraw and consider his options. 'Check out the gear. I'm going to speak to Mrs Webb. And don't fret that she's not trustworthy. She is. If it hadn't been for her this place would never have become the sanctuary it is.'

Sara looked painfully vulnerable as she stood watching him leave the room. But he wondered if he wasn't being the world's most gullible fool for taking her in. Or for being taken in by her? he mused, wanting to restore his sense of balance. He might be judging her husband without cause. But he didn't think he was. It might be foolish, but he trusted her.

But how the hell was he supposed to write fiction in his present frame of mind?

CHAPTER EIGHT

SARA spent the rest of the morning in her room, trying to come to terms with what Matt had told her.

Max wasn't dead, she repeated incredulously. He was alive. The fears she'd had on his behalf had been groundless. He'd been taken to hospital, sure, but he'd been well enough to discharge himself the following morning. And since then he'd been trying to cover himself by pretending that *she* had disappeared, that *she* might have been kidnapped.

She trembled. After Matt had left her, she'd taken up a position on the window seat, gazing out at the sun-drenched cliffs and the water beyond with a feeling of disbelief. She still found it hard to accept that she was here, hundreds of miles from London; that she'd escaped. However grateful she was that Max had survived, the manner of her departure remained a constant source of amazement. How had he let her get away?

Of course, he had been unconscious at the time. He must have hit his head when he fell and for a few minutes he'd been dead to the world. Dead to her, too, she thought bitterly. She should have known it would take more than a simple fall to kill a man like Max Bradbury.

Not that she wanted him dead, she assured herself. That was too high a price to pay, even for her freedom. But if only he had been a reasonable man, a man she could appeal to. When it had become obvious that their marriage was not what he had expected, that *she* was not what he had expected, why couldn't he have let her go? It was what any other man would have done; any normal man, that was. But it hadn't taken her long to find out that Max was anything but normal.

She supposed they must have been married for about six months when he'd struck her for the first time.

She'd already learned not to contradict him, particularly if he'd been drinking. He had said some incredibly cruel things to her, things he'd said he regretted bitterly when he was sober again, and she'd believed him. The crude words he'd used, deriding her for the smallest thing, belittling her intelligence, accusing her of being something she was not, had seemed so uncharacteristic of the man she'd believed she'd married. She'd been sure that it was the alcohol that was responsible for his ungovernable rage, and for a while he'd been able to hide his real nature from her.

But then everything had changed. It had only taken the discovery that she was on first-name terms with the commissionaire who worked in the lobby of their apartment building to invoke an almost insane fury. She'd been totally unprepared for the fist that had suddenly bored into her midriff and she'd been doubled over, gasping for air and sanity, when he'd stormed out of the duplex.

Of course, he'd apologised when he'd come back. He'd made the excuse of stress at the office, of being madly jealous of any man who spoke to her, of his own uncontrollable temper. He'd sworn it would never happen again, showered her with expensive presents until she'd been convinced of his regret.

Until the next time...

But she didn't want to think about that now; didn't want to consider what a naïve fool she had been, or how easily Max had managed to persuade her that she was actually to blame for his outbursts. In the beginning, desperate to make her marriage work—for her mother's sake as well as her own—she'd seized any excuse to explain his violence. The truth was, she hadn't been able to believe what was happening to her. She'd deluded herself that once Max realised she wasn't interested in any other man he'd come to his senses.

It hadn't happened. The violence had just got worse and there'd been nothing she could do. Max had made it very clear that he would never let her go, and she'd had the very real fear that if she did try to free herself he would turn his anger on her mother.

She was glad now that they'd had no children. Max would have had no compunction about using them in his unequal struggle for possession. Besides which, she realised now that his jealousy would never have allowed a third person to dilute the complete submission he demanded of her.

Thrusting these thoughts aside, she got to her feet and crossed to the small pile of clothes Matt had left on the loveseat. There were jeans, which she judged might fit her very well, a couple of tee shirts, two changes of cheap underwear, the kind that was available in supermarkets, and a pair of trainers.

She pressed her lips together after she had examined the clothes, her eyes filling with tears suddenly at his kindness. This presumably was the 'gift' he'd brought her, only to find her cowering behind the bathroom door. She'd been so afraid of him seeing her, of him finding out what Max had done to her, but now she was glad he knew. It was such a relief to have someone she could talk to, someone who wouldn't judge her. And, although she'd admitted nothing, she suspected Matt knew exactly what had been going on.

Sooner or later, she knew, she would have to go back, but please God not yet. Whatever excuse she gave, Max was never going to believe her version of events. Apart from anything else, she had shamed and humiliated him—or at least that was how he would see it. He was never going to forgive her for that.

Trying to ignore the inevitable, Sara carried the jeans and one of the tee shirts into the bathroom and took off her dress. The voile dress had been new, bought to go to the art exhibition Max had been planning to visit the evening when fate had overtaken both of them. It was strange to think it was the dress that had led to Max's accident. But then, it was on such simple things as these that her marriage had foundered.

As she hung the dress on the back of the bathroom door she thought how foolish she'd been to think that Max might like it. He hadn't chosen it, and for a long time now he had chosen all her clothes. But he had encouraged her to attend the fashion show with the wife of one of his colleagues, and, after seeing it modelled, Sara had fallen in love with its style and elegance.

Its style and elegance! Sara's lips curled in painful remembrance. Max hadn't thought it was either stylish or elegant. He'd said it was the kind of dress only a tart would wear, that she'd chosen it because she'd wanted to flaunt herself. She was quite sure that if he hadn't fallen down the stairs he'd have torn the garment off her, and she wished now that she'd taken the time to grab a change of clothes before fleeing from the apartment. She didn't like the dress now; she hated it. She took a breath. Hated *him*! God help her.

The jeans were a little big, but that didn't matter. At least they weren't tight on her hip. The tee shirt was cropped and ended a daring inch above her navel, which she worried about a little. But then she remembered Max wasn't going to see her. For now she could please herself what she wore.

The trainers fitted beautifully. Sara guessed Matt must have checked the size of her shoes before buying them. Whatever, she looked infinitely better. She felt almost her old self as she went downstairs at lunchtime.

The first person she encountered was Mrs Webb. The housekeeper was setting the table in the dining room again and Sara halted uncertainly, not sure she wanted to face another grilling.

But Mrs Webb had seen her and, straightening, she arched her brows appreciatively. 'You look nice,' she said, with none of the animosity that she'd exhibited earlier. 'Matt's got good taste.'

Sara gave a rueful smile, realising there was no point in pretending that she'd brought the garments with her. 'Where is— Matt?' she asked, for want of anything else to say, and the housekeeper returned to her task.

'He's in his office, study, whatever you want to call it.' She sounded indulgent. 'He said to tell you to go ahead and have lunch without him. I believe he's got a lot of work to catch up on, and he's got to pick Rosie up at three o'clock.'

Sara came a little further into the room. 'I didn't realise he was writing a book at the moment,' she said, feeling a familiar sense of inadequacy. 'I should apologise. I've taken up so much of his time.'

'Did I say he was complaining?' The older woman gave her a sideways glance. 'If you ask me, he's more than happy to have you here. Writing can be a lonely existence. And since Hester retired he's had to make do with Rosie's and my company.'

'Hester.' Sara remembered the little girl mentioning that name yesterday afternoon when she'd been trying to prove how grown up she was. 'Who—who is Hester?'

'She used to be Rosie's nanny,' explained Mrs Webb, straightening from the table again. 'She came north with Matt when he bought this place. She was from around here originally, just as he was.'

Sara nodded. 'But she left?'

'She retired,' replied the housekeeper, heading for the door. 'Now, you sit yourself down. I'll be back in a minute with your meal.'

Sara would have liked to ask if she could just have her meal in the kitchen, as she'd done the day before, but she was chary of getting too familiar with Mrs Webb. She didn't know what Matt had told her, if anything, and until she did it was probably safer to maintain a certain detachment.

The housekeeper returned with an appetising dish of lasagne and new bread, fresh out of the oven. She advised Sara to help herself and, although her appetite had been virtually non-existent since she left London, Sara found to her surprise that she was hungry.

She refused the glass of wine Mrs Webb offered, however. A diet cola was far more appealing, and by the time the house-keeper returned to see how she was doing she'd made a modest dent in the pasta.

'That was delicious,' she said, feeling pleased with herself. 'Did you make it?'

'Well, I didn't buy it,' remarked Mrs Webb drily. 'I don't hold with all those ready-made meals, although I suppose if you're a working girl you can't always spend half the day in the kitchen, can you?'

'No, I suppose not.'

Sara thought longingly of those occasions when she'd made a meal for her mother and herself. But that was in the days before Max came on the scene; before he'd come to the school to present a cheque to the governors to equip a new gymnasium and decided she was going to be the next Mrs Bradbury. Before Sara's mother had seen him as her last chance to escape from what she regarded as the near-poverty that had dogged her married life.

'So—can I get you anything else?' asked Mrs Webb, gathering the plates together. 'Some ice cream, perhaps?'

'Nothing else, thanks.' Sara took a deep breath, once again dispelling Max's image from her mind. 'Do you think Matt would mind if I took the dogs for a walk?'

The housekeeper looked surprised. 'I'd say he'd be delighted,' she replied drily. 'But are you sure you can manage them on your own? They're pretty wild.'

'I'm not as helpless as I look,' declared Sara with a smile. 'But I won't go down to the beach. I'm not that stupid.'

'Well, actually, you could now,' said the older woman thoughtfully. 'The tide's turned.'

Sara hoped so; she really did. But she wasn't thinking about the water that had trapped her earlier.

She accompanied Mrs Webb into the kitchen, helping her to load the lunch dishes into the dishwasher before going out into the garden. The two retrievers in their compound, sensing an outing, immediately set up a noisy greeting which completely masked the arrival of the young woman who suddenly appeared around the corner of the house.

Sara didn't know who was the most shocked: herself, because of her fear of being recognised, or the other woman, who clearly wasn't pleased to find her there. Sara didn't know how she knew the stranger didn't approve of her presence. She just sensed it. So who was she?

Mrs Webb supplied the answer. Following Sara out of the house, she saw the newcomer almost as soon as Sara did herself, and her lips parted in a pleasant smile.

'Mrs Proctor,' she said. 'What a surprise!'

The young woman came towards them. In a cream silk shirt tied stylishly at her waist and pleated linen trousers in a subtle shade of taupe she made Sara instantly aware of the limitations of her own attire. Mrs Proctor's hair was dark, a smooth silken cap that tucked confidingly beneath a most attractive chin. Sara guessed, too, that the hazel eyes set in a flawlessly oval face would miss little.

But for now the woman was obliged to acknowledge the housekeeper's greeting. Sara thought it was lucky that she hadn't let the dogs out. Mrs Proctor didn't look the type to appreciate having their paws on her clothes, and she ignored them as she produced an answering smile. 'Hello, Mrs Webb,' she said politely. 'Isn't it a perfect afternoon?'

And it was, thought Sara, glancing up at the clear blue sky above their heads. She just hoped the newcomer wasn't going to spoil it.

The realisation that she had no right to think things like that brought her up short. For heaven's sake, she chided herself, she probably had less right to be here than anyone else. In fact, scrub 'probably'. She had no right to be here at all.

'Is Matt working?'

Mrs Proctor's voice matched the rest of her: cool and cultivated, yet with an underlying note of arrogance. Sara had the impression she didn't care much for Mrs Webb either. But she was obliged to be civil.

'Yes, I'm afraid so.' Mrs Webb had brought the dogs' slip collars out with her, and now she handed them over to Sara. 'Is there anything I can do?'

In a pig's eye, thought Sara drily, guessing that the visitor would want nothing from the housekeeper. But it wasn't anything to do with her, and, dipping her head, she went to unbolt the compound gate.

'You're not going to let them out, are you?' Before Sara could open the gate, the woman stopped her. 'I mean—' She glanced down at her immaculate appearance. 'I really wish you wouldn't.'

Sara looked at Mrs Webb, and the older woman gestured resignedly towards the house. 'Perhaps you'd better come in then, Mrs Proctor,' she said, without enthusiasm. 'Maybe you'd like a cup of coffee before you leave.'

There was definite annoyance in the young woman's expression now, but she controlled it. 'That might be very nice,' she agreed, but her gaze had returned to linger curiously on Sara. 'I didn't realise Matt employed someone to exercise the dogs for him.' She wet her already glossy lips. 'Are you a local, Miss—Miss—?'

'She's from the agency.'

Matt's interjection caught them all unawares. Sara had assumed he was still closeted in his study and she was disturbed at how eagerly her eyes turned to him.

He was still wearing the black tee shirt and jeans he'd been wearing when he'd come into her bedroom, and, although she hadn't realised it at the time, his appearance had registered with her. The dark colour accentuated his raw masculinity, drew her unwilling attention to the impressive width of his chest, to the powerful muscles in his thighs. Looking at him, she could hardly believe how gentle he had been with her, how sensual his lips had felt against her skin...

But then what he'd said registered, too, and she dipped her head again, unable to meet his eyes. Dear God, was he offering her the job as Rosie's nanny? And, if so, what did she intend to do?

'I told you I was still looking for a nanny, didn't I, Emma?' Matt continued, addressing his remarks to the visitor. 'Meet Miss Sara Victor. We're giving each other a week's trial to see how it goes.'

Emma!

As Sara realised that this must be the woman who'd phoned Matt the day before, Emma Proctor looked decidedly put out. 'I thought you said that you hadn't seen any suitable applicants,' she exclaimed, giving Sara a disparaging look. 'This was rather sudden, wasn't it?'

'Isn't that always the way?' remarked Matt with amazing sanguinity. 'Sara just arrived yesterday.'

'She's very good with Rosie,' put in Mrs Webb, not to be outdone, and Sara wished they'd stop talking about her as if she wasn't there. Though she had no wish to draw attention to herself, she reminded herself firmly. And she could hardly object if Mrs Webb was sticking up for her.

'That's true,' Matt added now, but Sara noticed he raked a restless hand through his hair as he spoke. Perhaps he wasn't as relaxed about this as he appeared, she fretted anxiously. And was it fair to expect him to cover for her this way?

Meanwhile Emma Proctor was doing her best to hide her resentment and, ignoring Sara completely, she remarked, 'Mrs Webb told me you were working.' She treated the housekeeper to the kind of look she'd given Sara earlier. 'I was hoping you'd have time for a chat. I've been meaning to ask you about the books you said you'd sign for Darren's school fête.'

Matt's smile looked a little forced now. 'Well, I am working, Em—'

'But you're not working right now, are you?' she pointed out smoothly, with another impatient glance at Sara and Mrs Webb. 'It will only take a minute. And I have driven over specially.'

Matt took a deep breath. 'Okay,' he said, apparently accepting defeat. 'You'd better come in.'

Mrs Webb pulled a wry face at Sara as Emma went triumphantly up the steps and into the bootroom, and Sara felt an unexpected sense of camaraderie with the older woman. But when she started towards the dogs again Matt caught her arm.

'What are you doing?'

'Miss Victor asked if she could take the dogs for a walk,' said Mrs Webb, before Sara could respond. 'That's all right, isn't it?'

'No, it's not all right,' he retorted, and Sara, who had been momentarily struck dumb by the possessiveness of his strong fingers, shook herself free.

'Why not?' she demanded, aware that Emma Proctor had paused to listen to their exchange. Her eyes challenged his. 'I've got nothing to do until Rosie comes home.'

'Because you're not familiar with the area,' he said tersely, clearly aware of his audience. 'You can come with Rosie and me when we take them out later.'

'But—'

'I doubt if—Miss Victor, is it?—is likely to lose her bearings around here,' observed Emma Proctor, once again reminding him of her presence. 'This is the only house along this stretch of the coast.'

'Even so—'

Matt didn't say anything more, but his expression was compelling and Sara knew she couldn't go against him. He was sticking his neck out by allowing her to stay here, and the least she could do was respect his wishes.

'Okay,' she said, with a small shrug. Then, because she couldn't resist it, 'I suppose I'll have to go and pick Rosie up in a little while anyway.'

Matt's expression mirrored his impatience. 'We'll talk about that,' he stated flatly, and although his eyes promised a suitable retribution Sara wasn't alarmed. He followed Emma up the steps and into the house. 'I won't be long.'

Sara's lips twitched, and after Matt and Emma had disappeared she turned back to the dogs with a rueful smile. 'Sorry, guys,' she said, squatting down on her heels and pushing her fingers through the bars. 'You're going to have to wait. We all are.'

'You're staying on, then, are you?'

Mrs Webb's enquiry reminded Sara that there'd been a fourth witness to their exchange. 'For a short time,' she said, getting to her feet again. Then, because she had to know, 'What has he told you?'

'Me?' For the first time the housekeeper looked a little taken aback. 'Matt doesn't have to clear his arrangements with me.'

'I know, but—' Sara sought for words. 'He must have said something.'

Mrs Webb folded her hands together at her waist. 'As I say, he doesn't have to tell me anything. If he says you're going to be Rosie's nanny, then that's good enough for me.'

Sara sighed. 'Mrs Webb—'

'All right.' The housekeeper gave in. 'He asked me not to gossip about your arrival. I know you're in some kind of trouble, and he's trying to help you, but that's all. I trust Matt to know what he's doing. He is a trained psychologist, you know.'

Sara's eyes had widened. 'A trained psychologist?' she echoed. 'He didn't tell me that.'

'No, well, it's not something he likes me to gossip about either,' said Mrs Webb drily. 'Now, I must get on…'

'Why did he give it up?' asked Sara, unable to stop herself, and the housekeeper sighed.

'Can't you guess? To pursue his writing career, of course. Rosie was just a baby at the time.'

Sara bit her lip. 'Was that—was that when his wife left him?'

'Miss Victor—'

'Call me Sara, please!'

'Sara, then.' Mrs Webb folded her lips together for a moment before continuing, 'Don't you think you ought to ask Matt these questions, not me?'

Sara flushed, but she stood her ground. 'I'm sorry,' she said a little stiffly. 'I didn't mean to pry.'

'No—' Mrs Webb turned towards the house, only to pause with her foot on the bottom step. 'I don't suppose it will do any harm to tell you that Carol—that's his ex-wife—wasn't prepared to give up the comfortable existence she'd had as a doctor's wife. There was no certainty Matt would have any success as a writer.'

'But she left her baby behind,' protested Sara, unable to conceive of any woman doing such a thing, and the housekeeper nodded.

'Yes, well, she married one of Matt's partners in the practice just a week after their divorce became absolute,' she conceded with a grimace. 'Rosie would have been in the way.'

Then, as if she realising she had already said too much, Mrs Webb disappeared into the house.

CHAPTER NINE

MATT stared at the blank computer screen in front of him and scowled. For the first time in his writing career he was finding it almost impossible to concentrate on his work, and it irritated the hell out of him.

He knew what was wrong with him, of course. He was getting far too involved in Sara's life. Despite the fact that he'd promised her not to say or do anything to alert Max Bradbury to her whereabouts, the temptation to let the bastard know exactly what he thought of him was hard to resist. More than that, he itched to bury his fist in Bradbury's face, which was totally unlike him.

He'd always considered himself a reasonable man. Hell, when Carol had first left him and shacked up with Philip Arnold he'd never even thought of resorting to violence. Which probably said more about his relationship with his ex-wife than his own character, he conceded ruefully. In all honesty, if it hadn't been for Rosie they'd have probably split up long before they had.

So what did that say about the present situation? Why did he feel this overpowering need to protect Sara? And what had possessed him to tell Emma Proctor that she was Rosie's new nanny? By now the news was probably common knowledge throughout the county.

Yet, during the three days that had passed since Emma's visit, he had to admit that the demands on his time had been eased. Although he hadn't allowed Sara to pick Rosie up from school, there was no doubt that she had taken much of the responsibility for entertaining his daughter once she was home off his shoulders.

Of course, Sara wasn't a nanny. But he believed her story about being a teacher now. She was good with the little girl and Rosie liked her. In normal circumstances he'd have con-

sidered himself very lucky to have her, but these circumstances
were anything but normal.

His scowl deepened. One of his main sources of discontent
was the fact that Sara had resisted all his efforts to find out why
she stayed with her husband. She insisted that in a few more
days she would have to go back, and that was the real cause of
his writer's block. Why did she feel any allegiance towards
him? What twisted hold did the man have over her life?

Dammit! Leaving his desk, he walked to the windows, looking out on the scene that usually never failed to soothe his
troubled psyche. The North Sea was grey today, reflecting the
clouds that hovered over the headland. The mournful sound of
a ship's foghorn seemed to echo his mood, and he lifted both
hands to massage the taut muscles at the back of his neck.

He had to stop this, he told himself savagely. He had to stop
behaving as if he had any role to play in Sara's future. Despite
that emotional scene in her bedroom, when he'd made such a
pathetic fool of himself, their association remained very much
that of an employer and an employee. She'd accepted his excuse
for staying on with obvious gratitude, but there'd been no further intimacy between them. Indeed, there were times when
Matt wondered if he'd imagined the whole thing.

But then he'd remember the bruises he'd seen on her body
and know he hadn't.

He swore again, balling a fist and pressing it hard against the
windowframe. He increased the pressure until all the blood had
left his fingers and his hand was numb. And then, with an angry
exclamation, he withdrew it and thrust it into his pocket, finding
a masochistic pleasure in the pain he'd inflicted upon himself.

At least he'd done as he'd promised and let Bradbury know
that his wife was safe and well. Or as safe and well as a woman
who'd been brutalised could be, he amended grimly. He had a
friend at the *London Chronicle* and he'd merely called in a
favour by getting him to deliver the note Sara had written. Of
course he hadn't told her that he'd made the note public property, but there'd been no way he could have risked Max
Bradbury burying it and continuing with his bogus concern.

As it was, there'd been a small item in yesterday's papers.

News of the letter had evidently circulated round the tabloid editors, as he'd hoped it would, and Bradbury had had to come up with a convincing explanation.

His story was that the blow he'd suffered to his head when he fell had temporarily robbed him of his memory. Thanks to Matt's friend, he was able to claim that he'd contacted the *Chronicle* himself, as soon as he'd remembered that Victoria had told him she was going to visit a schoolfriend in the north of England. He'd had a letter from her now, he said, and all was well.

Until she went back, thought Matt, feeling his muscles tighten again. He'd probably done her no favours by holding Bradbury's name up to possible ridicule, but it was too late now. It was just something else 'Victoria' would have to pay for.

Victoria!

His jaw clenched. One thing she had told him was that Victoria wasn't her real name. She'd been christened Sara, she said, and Matt could only assume that it hadn't been sophisticated enough for Max Bradbury's wife. Not that she'd complained about it to him. Despite the fear she obviously had of her husband, she was absurdly loyal. Even though she must know that by changing her name he had removed another of the props that had made her who she was.

Matt had decided not to show Sara the article in the newspaper. He hadn't wanted her to be concerned because Bradbury had implied that he knew where she was. The fact that he'd chosen to tell the media that she was in the north of England was just a coincidence. It had to be. But it was another example of how everything seemed to work to Bradbury's advantage.

Sara's rental car was no longer advertising her presence, at least. He'd had the garage in Saviour's Bay pick it up and return it to the local franchise in Ellsmoor, and, although he'd been forced to admit that there'd been nothing wrong with it in the first place, Sara hadn't complained. Whatever she chose to do after she left here, for the moment she seemed happy to be free of all obligations.

The phone rang before he could indulge in any further introspection, and, tamping down his resentment, he went to answer it.

'Yeah?'

'Matt?'

He recognised the voice at once. It was his agent, Rob Marco, and he pulled a wry face. He could guess what Rob wanted: some kind of timeframe for the completion of the new manuscript. The fact that he should have been in the final stages by now was just another cause for his tension.

'Hi, Rob,' he answered now, dropping down into his leather chair and propping his feet on the edge of his desk. He glanced at his watch. 'How are things with you?'

'They could be better,' replied Rob, with just the trace of an edge to his voice. 'How are things with you, Matt? When can I expect the new manuscript?'

Matt gave a sardonic snort. 'I should have guessed this wasn't a social call,' he said, hooking the phone between his ear and his shoulder and pulling open the bottom drawer of the desk. 'I don't work well with deadlines, Rob. You know that.'

There was a moment's silence while the other man considered his response and Matt used it to lift the half-empty bottle of whisky from the drawer. Unscrewing the cap, he treated himself to a healthy swig before setting it down beside the computer. He deserved some consolation, he told himself defensively. It was lunchtime, after all, and problems were assaulting him on all sides.

'I'm not giving you a deadline,' said Rob at last, his tone infinitely more conciliatory. 'But, as you know, your next book is due for publication in the spring. Your publishers would just like to be able to announce the date of publication of the new novel on the flyleaf.'

'What you mean is, they're hoping I'll sign a new contract,' remarked Matt drily. 'Have they come to you with any figures? I assume they've got an offer in mind?'

Rob sighed. 'We haven't gone into specifics, Matt. I wouldn't do that without your say-so. But Nash is a good publisher. They've done pretty well by you in the past.'

'In other words, you're interested,' said Matt, studying the

toes of his loafers. Rob was a good agent, and if he was rec-
ommending another deal it meant Nash had come up with a
pretty spectacular sum. Of course, the book Nash was hoping
to negotiate for wasn't his current work in progress. Their interest had been prompted by his next project, an outline of
which had been with his publishers for the past three weeks.

'It's inviting,' affirmed Rob. 'I doubt if you'd get a better
offer.' He paused. 'They're hoping they can persuade you to
sign a three-book deal this time. They're talking seven figures.
That's as much as I'm going to say.'

Matt shook his head. 'Seven figures,' he echoed wryly, wishing he felt more enthusiasm for Rob's news. But right now
getting his current manuscript finished and ready for despatch
seemed an insurmountable task. The idea of committing himself
to writing three more books, even with a seven-figure advance,
sounded almost impossible to achieve.

'What's wrong?' Rob was nothing if not intuitive. 'Isn't it
enough?'

'More than enough,' responded Matt, blowing out a breath.
'Thanks, Rob. As I've said before, you're the best agent in the
business.'

'But you're not happy.' Rob wasn't deceived. 'Come on,
Matt. What's your problem? Is it Rosie?'

'Rosie's fine.' Matt chose to answer his last question first.

'You got her a nanny, right?'

Matt hesitated. 'Not exactly.'

'Not exactly?' Rob was curious. 'What's that supposed to
mean? Either you got her a nanny or you didn't.'

Matt wished he'd just answered in the negative and been
done with it. 'I've got a temporary nanny,' he said at last. Then,
hoping Rob would take the hint, 'Thanks for calling, Rob. I'll
be in touch as soon as I have some definite news.'

Rob sounded put out. 'Is that all you're going to say?' he
exclaimed. 'You haven't even told me how the new manuscript
is coming along.'

'It's getting there,' said Matt evasively. 'I'm sorry if you
think I'm ungrateful. I've got a lot on my plate at the moment.'

'Including the temporary nanny?' suggested Rob shrewdly.

'Who is she, Matt? A girlfriend? I tell you, pal, that's not a good idea. You should never mix business with pleasure.'

If only he could, thought Matt bitterly, and then chided himself for the thought. Just because Sara was grateful for his protection it did not mean she spent her time fantasising about what *he'd* be like in bed. After her experiences, sex would be the last thing on her mind. Besides, however unhappily, she was married. And at no time had she let him think that anything else was on the cards.

It was pathetic. *He* was pathetic, he thought irritably. At the first opportunity he should find himself another woman and get a life. There was always Emma. Since her husband had died she'd made no secret of the fact that she'd be willing to advance their relationship. But he wasn't attracted to Emma; he hadn't been attracted to anyone for a long time. So why the hell was Sara Bradbury playing havoc with his hormones?

'It's nothing like that,' he told Rob shortly. 'She's just someone I met recently who was looking for a job. But she's not staying. As I said before, it's just a temporary arrangement. But Rosie likes her. And that's what matters.'

'So what's she like?' Rob was trying to sound casual and failing abysmally. He'd probably made the connection between his evasion and Sara's arrival, thought Matt grimly. 'Is she young? Attractive? Married?'

A knock at the study door interrupted Matt's concentration. 'Come in,' he called impatiently, guessing it was Mrs Webb with a sandwich for his lunch. Then, to Rob. 'I'm not getting into what she looks like. She's—passable, okay? But in any case she doesn't interest me.'

It was only as he was completing this sentence that he looked up and realised it wasn't the housekeeper who was hovering in the doorway. With an inward groan, he let his eyes meet Sara's across the width of the room. She had evidently heard what he was saying to Rob and taken exception to it. He was devastated by the injured look that crossed her face.

'Ah. Damn—' His exclamation was audible to both Sara and Rob, but he didn't have time to spare his agent's feelings right now. 'Speak to you later, Rob,' he said quickly. 'Something's come up.' And, slamming down the phone, he got to his feet. 'Sara—'

'You didn't have to do that,' she said, the stiffness of her words only equalled by the rigidity of her stance. Matt closed his eyes for a moment against the almost irresistible impulse he had to leap across his desk and take her in his arms. 'I could have come back.'

She looked so delicate standing there, so fragile. Only yesterday he'd thought she was losing that look of vulnerability; that the time she'd spent outdoors with Rosie and the dogs had added a glow of health to her pale skin. She was still far too thin, of course, but her appetite was definitely improving. She'd been gaining in confidence, too. He could have sworn it.

Now his careless words had spoiled everything. And he could hardly tell her he'd only said what he had to put Rob off the scent. She wouldn't want to know why he'd said it. It wasn't her fault that she was having such a stressful effect on his life.

'Sara—' he began again, but she wouldn't let him finish.

'I only came to ask if you'd like your lunch now,' she continued, in the same unyielding tone. 'I heard the phone and it seemed a good opportunity to interrupt you.'

'I don't mind—'

'That's all right, then, isn't it?' She took a breath. 'I'll get your tray. Mrs Webb left it ready.'

'Dammit!' Matt swore. He'd forgotten that the housekeeper had told him she had a dental appointment at twelve o'clock. 'There's no need for you to run around after me. I don't expect it. I'm not your husband.'

'No, you're not.'

Sara was already retreating through the door when Matt went after her. He didn't know what had made him say what he had, but it was obvious she'd been hurt by his words. The trouble was, it was becoming more and more difficult not to show how he was feeling, and he wished he could explain it to her.

He caught her in the hall outside his study, his hand closing round her arm and bringing her to a halt. 'Sara,' he started again. 'I'm sorry if I was short with you. When Rob gets on the phone it's usually because he wants something that I can't give him.'

'I'm really not interested,' she said, making an effort to release herself from his hold, and Matt gave an impatient sigh.

'Listen to me,' he said. 'Rob Marco is my agent. He was ringing to ask why he hasn't had the new manuscript. I was making the excuse that I still didn't have a permanent nanny for Rosie.'

Sara's brows arched scornfully. 'So?'

'So that's why I said what I did,' exclaimed Matt doggedly. 'You probably thought I was criticising you. I wasn't, whatever it sounded like. I was just trying to distract Rob from his impression that you're really my girlfriend.'

'Look, I really don't care—'

'No, but I do,' muttered Matt, his patience wearing thin. 'I'm telling you the truth, dammit. If I'd finished the damn manuscript we wouldn't be having this conversation.'

'I hope you're not implying that I'm to blame for that,' she countered coldly, stiffening her back, and Matt expelled a long breath.

He was trying hard not to be aware of her small breasts rising and falling in tempo with her increasing indignation, the widening gap between her tee shirt and jeans exposing the intriguing hollow of her navel. She was so incredibly sexy, with her face flushed, her eyes sparkling with aggravated fire. He could feel a sensuous warmth spreading from his fingers to every erogenous nerve in his body, and he knew he was getting dangerously close to combustion.

'I didn't say that,' he said now, struggling to contain his frustration, and she uttered a triumphant snort.

'Good,' she said fiercely, and he had the sudden suspicion that she was using her anger to put a barrier between them. 'Because I suggest that bottle of whisky on your desk is far more culpable than me!'

Matt choked on an oath. 'Are you kidding?' he gasped. 'I've had one mouthful of Scotch and that's all.'

'So you say.'

'It's the truth.' He was aware of a growing sense of outrage. 'I'm not an alcoholic.'

'Well, it isn't even lunchtime yet,' she persisted, and he shook his head in angry disbelief.

'Where do you get off telling me what to do?' he demanded, using his free hand to pull her round to face him, and then could have died with mortification when he saw her flinch.

It was obvious that she had encountered this kind of situation before and she expected the worst. The look in her eyes damned and humiliated him, and with a groan of anguish he hauled her into his arms.

'God, I'm sorry,' he muttered, one hand cradling the back of her neck while the other circled her waist. Silky hair brushed his fingers and her skin was incredibly soft beneath his hands. 'Hell, Sara, don't you know I would never hurt you?'

Her response was muffled, but he could feel the sudden wetness that was dampening his shirt. She was crying, and her distress assaulted him like acid on an open wound. He felt so powerless; so useless. He wanted to help her, but all he was doing was turning her against him, too.

'Sara, Sara,' he breathed, his fingers caressing her nape, and she did the unforgivable and turned her face up to his.

Her eyes were flooded with tears, but her expression was more forgiving than accusatory. Lashes, several shades darker than her hair, sparkled with jewelled drops, and Matt's tongue itched to lick them away. She was so beautiful, so vulnerable, and the knowledge that he had no right to hold her like this was tearing him to pieces. Did she know what she was doing? he wondered. What she was doing to him? Of course she did, he assured himself. He was holding her too close for the swelling in his pants to be ignored.

Then, 'Matt,' she said huskily, and it was more than he could bear.

When her hand lifted to his face he caught it and brought her palm to his lips. But even that wasn't enough. He wanted her so much, wanted more than he had any right to expect, and he might never have another chance like this.

Her eyes were wide now, her lips parted and unknowingly

sensual. There was a moment when he might have drawn back, when he might have fought the demons that were riding him, but the sight of her tongue defeated him. When the pink tip appeared to circle her lips, he knew he had to taste it, and, cupping her face between his hands, he bent his head and kissed her.

'Forgive me,' he groaned, his tongue slipping into her mouth, and after only a momentary hesitation she yielded to his intimate caress.

He'd intended to be gentle with her. He was fairly sure that any relationship she'd had with her husband would not have been gentle, and he'd wanted there to be no confusion between who was holding her, who was kissing her now.

But the moment his mouth covered hers all reason deserted him. He was like a man in the desert who was suddenly presented with a flask of cool clear water and didn't realise until that moment that he was dying of thirst. Maybe it was the way her lips opened to his, or the sensuous brush of her tongue. Or perhaps the devastating realisation he had that she was kissing him back.

Whatever, at that moment all bets were off. The heat that flared between them was automatic and uncontrollable, and Matt's mind swam with the emotions she so easily aroused inside him. He was like a man possessed, and when she wound her arms around his waist and hooked her thumbs into his belt he swayed back against the wall behind him, taking her with him.

The blood was pounding in his head, thundering through his veins, making any kind of coherent thought impossible. She burrowed against him, making him overwhelmingly aware of the layers of fabric that divided them. His skin felt raw, sensitised. He had to fight the urge to peel her tee shirt from her and bury his face between her breasts.

His hands slid down her back as he continued to kiss her, lingering on the bare skin of her midriff that was so tantalisingly warm to his touch. The temptation to slide his hands beneath the tee shirt and caress the erect nipples that were straining the soft material was almost irresistible, but he dammed the impulse and cupped her rounded bottom instead.

Urging her against him was the purest form of torture, but it was worth it. Spreading his legs, he cradled her against the erection throbbing between his thighs. She rubbed herself against him and he wondered if she had any idea what she was inviting. How much more of this could he take without losing it completely?

And then she moaned.

It was a plaintive little sound, barely audible, in fact, but he heard it. For a moment he thought he'd hurt her. He was half afraid that his urgent hands had been too rough for her delicate skin. But then, with a shocking sense of his own insanity, he suddenly realised what was wrong.

With unsteady hands he managed to put some space between them, avoiding her eyes as he made some inane apology for touching her as he had. And all the while he chided himself for being a fool, for imagining that she had been as caught up in her emotions as he was. It wasn't true. That grotesque little moan had proved it. He'd been making love to a woman who had undoubtedly been conditioned never to say no...

CHAPTER TEN

'BUT why can't you stay?' Rosie gazed up at Sara with tear-filled eyes. 'I don't want you to go.'

'And I don't want to go,' said Sara, wondering if she was being entirely wise in admitting as much. But she hated lying to the child. 'I'm sorry, sweetheart. But this was just a temporary arrangement.'

'But why?' Rosie wouldn't let it go. 'You like it here. You said so. And I like you. Mrs Webb likes you. Even Daddy likes you.'

Does he?

Sara reserved judgement on that. Since that morning a couple of days ago, when Mrs Webb had gone to the dentist, Matt had barely spoken two words to her, and she was left with the unhappy conclusion that he regretted what had happened.

She regretted it, too, she reflected painfully, but for totally different reasons. Which was quite an admission to make, she conceded with a twinge of shame. Was she wicked for regretting that Matt hadn't gone on and finished what he'd started? Was it completely unforgivable to wish that for once in her miserable life she might have known the joy of a real man's love?

Only Matt didn't love her, she reminded herself swiftly. Once again she was deluding herself about the reason for his actions, just as she had deluded herself that Max had ever really cared about her. She was a pathetic creature, so desperate for affection that she was willing to do almost anything to prove that Max's estimation of her wasn't true.

And, until Matt had pushed her away from him and taken refuge in his study, she had believed that she might be happy here. For the first time in years she'd felt secure; wanted; almost content. It was only later that she'd wondered if she hadn't been deceiving herself all along. It wasn't the house or the circum-

stances of her employment that had made her feel secure. It was
Matt. Only Matt. And how sad was that?

'When are you leaving?'

Until Rosie spoke again Sara had been staring blindly out of
the window, but now she turned to the child with rueful eyes.
And felt even worse when she saw the tragic look on the little
girl's face.

'Well, not today,' she said with determined cheerfulness,
picking up a velour skirt and jacket that belonged to one of
Rosie's dolls and exhibiting it for her approval. 'What do you
think of this? Smart, or what?'

They were sitting on the floor of the family room, and until
Rosie had brought up the subject of Sara's employment again
they'd been sorting through the toy cupboard for things Rosie
could donate to the school fair.

Matt had collected his daughter from school a couple of
hours ago. Sara had been having a cup of tea with Mrs Webb
in the kitchen when they'd got back and Matt had merely de-
posited the little girl with them before heading back to his study.

'That man's overdoing it,' the housekeeper had remarked
sagely as Rosie helped herself to a biscuit from the tin. 'He's
looking tired, don't you think? I suppose it's because he's trying
to get as much done as he can before you have to go back to
London. He's going to miss you and that's a fact.'

Sara had made some non-committal comment, not wanting
to get into a discussion about Matt in front of the child. It was
only now she realised that, however distracted she'd seemed at
the time, Rosie missed very little.

As if to underline this thought, she scrambled to her feet now
and climbed onto the window seat. 'Shall we go for a walk?'

'A walk?' Sara looked up at her. 'But it will be supper time
soon.' She paused. 'Besides, I thought you wanted to tidy the
toy cupboard.'

'I can do that any time,' said Rosie, her small fingers making
damp circles on the glass. She glanced back with accusing eyes.
'When you're not here.'

Sara sighed. 'Oh, Rosie—'

'Well, can we? Go for a walk, I mean? We don't have to

take the dogs. Daddy took them out before I went to school this morning.'

'Did he?'

Sara hadn't known that. He must have taken them out incredibly early, she thought. She'd been up herself at seven o'clock.

'Daddy's always up early,' continued Rosie, getting down again and standing with her feet apart and her hands on her hips, staring at Sara. 'I'm never late for school these days.'

'Well, that's good,' said Sara, getting to her feet and smiling at the little girl. 'You don't want to be late, do you?'

'I don't care.' Rosie was deliberately offhand. 'I'll be going away to school soon, and then it won't matter.'

Sara blinked. 'Going away to school?' she echoed. 'Who told you that?'

Rosie shrugged, bundling all the toys and games they'd taken out back into the cupboard and closing the door. 'Are we going for a walk?'

'In a minute.' Sara wanted to know what Rosie had heard. 'Is that what your daddy says?'

Rosie was still offhand. 'Maybe.'

'What do you mean, maybe? Either he did or he didn't.'

Rosie pursed her lips. 'I heard him talking to Mrs Armstrong.'

Sara frowned. 'Mrs Armstrong? Is that your teacher?'

'No. My teacher's Mrs Sanders,' said Rosie scornfully. 'Mrs Armstrong is Rupert and Nigel's mother.'

'Oh, I see.' Sara assumed they must be children in her class. 'And—you heard your daddy telling Mrs Armstrong that you'd be going away to school soon? Is that right?'

'No.' Rosie started for the door. 'Can we go?'

Sara heaved a sigh. She had no right to question the child, but she wanted to know what Matt had been saying. It was obvious it was on Rosie's mind, and perhaps he ought to be told that it wasn't wise to discuss his daughter's future with—with whom? Who was this Mrs Armstrong? Apart from being Rupert and Nigel's mother, of course. Was she another woman, like Emma Proctor, who considered herself more than just a friend?

'We'll go when you tell me what you heard,' she declared firmly, and Rosie sniffed.

'Does it matter?'

'I think it might.'

Sara gazed at her solemnly, wishing she didn't have to be stern with her. Rosie looked so adorable in her white canvas shorts and striped tee shirt, and Sara was tempted to take her in her arms and hug her and tell her that Matt wouldn't dream of sending her away to school. But until she knew what had been said she had to tamp down her emotions, even if the little girl had found a special place in her heart.

'Oh—well…' Rosie was reluctant to go on. 'It was something Mrs Armstrong said, that's all.'

'Which was?'

'Well, she said Daddy hadn't been very lucky with nannies,' mumbled Rosie unwillingly. 'That when you left he'd likely have to send me away.'

'She said that!' Sara was appalled.

'Not 'xactly.'

'Well, what *exactly* did she say?' demanded Sara, and then felt her face flood with hot colour when she suddenly realised that Matt was standing in the open doorway.

He must have heard what they were saying, she thought, a sinking feeling in her stomach. Oh, God, he was going to think she'd been pumping the child for information. He might even think she was curious about this Mrs Armstrong, whoever she was. And just because he might be right that was no excuse.

'What's going on?' he asked, his gaze moving between them, and Sara and Rosie exchanged an embarrassed look.

The little girl recovered herself first. 'We were just talking about school, Daddy,' she said, with remarkable aplomb. 'Now we're going for a walk.'

'Wait a minute.' Sara thought she should have known that Matt wouldn't swallow that. 'I think you should go and check with Mrs Webb first. She may have something she wants you to do.'

'Like what?'

Rosie was indignant, but her father's expression warned her not to argue. With a hunching of her shoulders she marched out of the door, leaving Sara to face the music alone.

Matt waited until his daughter was out of earshot and then arched an enquiring brow. 'School?' he said, without inflection. 'What have you been telling her?'

'Me?' Despite the quickening of her heartbeat, Sara managed to sound reasonably calm. 'I haven't been telling her anything. Well, not about school anyway.'

Matt came further into the room. He was wearing shorts today, khaki shorts that exposed his long muscled legs. Like hers, his black tee shirt barely skimmed his waistband, and her eyes were unwillingly drawn to the wedge of brown skin that appeared every time he moved.

Why was it that when she looked at him she was so acutely aware of her own sexuality? she wondered. Why, when for years she'd believed herself immune from any man's attraction, was she so irresistibly drawn to Matt's masculine grace? It was pointless, when all was said and done, and foolish. But she couldn't help herself. And if Max ever found out...

Well, he'd make her suffer for it, she reflected bitterly. But then, he'd make her suffer anyway. And perhaps she deserved his contempt. She was his wife, after all. She shouldn't be having these kinds of feelings for a man who wasn't her husband. Yet it was such a long time since Max had engendered anything inside her but fear and revulsion.

Even thinking about what was facing her when she returned to London was terrifying. Max was never going to forgive her for leaving him as she had. She mustn't forget that he knew that she was to blame for his fall. However accidental it might have been, she would bear the brunt of his wrath.

'So what were you talking about?'

Matt's words broke into her pained reverie and she forced herself to meet his dark gaze. Was that an accusation she could see in the depths of his eyes? Or was it just, as Mrs Webb had said, that he did look excessively weary?

She hesitated now, and then, deciding she had nothing to

lose, she said quietly, 'Are you thinking of sending Rosie away to school?'

'What?'

He looked stunned, and Sara felt somewhat reassured. 'You're not?'

'What the hell are you talking about?' he demanded, and then, as if noting how his angry words affected her, he calmed down. 'Where did you get that idea?'

'Would you believe from Rosie?' Sara dug her fingers into the back pockets of her jeans, aware that her hands were sweating. She wished she had shorts to wear, she thought ruefully. The jeans were far too warm for the humid weather they were having at present. But beggars couldn't be choosers. 'I think she's worried about what you're planning to do when I leave.'

'Rosie?' Matt shook his head. 'But I've never—'

'Not even to Mrs Armstrong?' asked Sara, before she lost her nerve, and Matt's eyes narrowed.

'Gloria?' he said, apparently confirming that he knew the woman far better than Sara could have wished.

'If that's her name,' she agreed, annoyed to hear the note of censure in her voice. 'I believe you were discussing the problems you were having in keeping a nanny with her.'

'Blast!' Matt raised a hand and raked long fingers over his scalp. His action widened the gap between his shirt and his shorts and once again Sara's eyes were drawn to his flat stomach. 'What did Rosie say?'

'What? Oh—' Sara swallowed, finding it difficult to drag her gaze away from his taut body. Trying to concentrate on what she was saying, she mumbled, 'I don't remember exactly what she said now.'

'No?' Matt didn't sound convinced, and, as if becoming aware of her distraction, he uttered a rough oath. Turning away from her, he added in a strangled voice, 'Dammit, Sara, will you stop looking at me that way? It's difficult enough keeping my hands off you as it is.'

Sara sucked in her breath. She'd never expected that. 'I'm sorry,' she said huskily. She turned towards the door. 'Would you like me to go?'

Matt gave an incredulous snort. 'No, I wouldn't like you to go,' he retorted harshly. 'I think you know what I'd really like you to do, so don't let's pretend we're fooling anybody here. You're married, and for some crazy reason you insist on going back to your husband. I can't say I'm happy about it, but my feelings don't count for much, do they?'

'Matt—'

'Don't,' he advised her grimly, putting the width of the room between them. Then, squaring his shoulders, he turned back to face her. 'Now, tell me what you know about my conversation with Gloria.'

Sara licked her dry lips. She didn't want to talk about Gloria Armstrong, she thought impatiently. What she really wanted was for Matt to tell her how he really felt about her being here. Yet, as he'd said, she had no right to expect anything more from him. He'd done what he could to help her and that ought to be enough.

But it wasn't. She wanted so much more.

He was waiting for her answer, and her heart gave an odd little flutter at the strangely vulnerable look on his face. He was a tall man, strong and virile, his dark hair tumbled by the restless invasion of his hands. Even with the shadow of stubble on his jawline and his mouth set in a grim line he set her pulses racing. She had no fear of him. He'd taught her that strength could be tempered not with violence, but love.

But she couldn't tell him that. Shaking her head, she struggled to remember what they'd been talking about before she'd been distracted. 'I—I've told you all I know,' she submitted at last. And then, to assuage her own frustration, she added, 'Is Mrs Armstrong another of your admirers?'

'Another of my—' Matt's eyes darkened. 'I don't have admirers, Sara. Gloria Armstrong's husband farms the land north of here. They have two boys who are in Rosie's class.'

Sara lifted her shoulders. 'I see.'

'Do you?' Matt turned away from her again and stared broodingly out of the window. 'What did you think? That I have a covey of women I can call on when I want to get laid?'

Sara couldn't prevent herself. 'And do you?'

'Oh, sure.' Matt scowled at her over his shoulder. 'I'm a regular stud!'

Sara pressed her lips together, not sure how to take him now. 'Why doesn't that surprise me?' she muttered, and he made an exasperated sound.

'I won't dignify that comment with a response,' he stated harshly. 'Dammit, Sara, don't you know me better than that? And before you start on Emma, I'll tell you that she and I are just good friends.'

'Her husband, too?'

'What's it to you?' Matt swung round. Then, as if taking pity on her, he made an impatient gesture. 'She's a widow,' he said. 'Her husband was killed in a car crash about two years ago, leaving her with a ten-year-old son to raise on her own.'

Sara frowned. 'This would be—Darren, yes?'

'You don't miss much, do you?' Matt was ironic. 'But, yeah. Darren's her son.'

'I suppose—I suppose she depends on you,' ventured Sara cautiously, not quite sure where she was going with this. 'Are you—very close?'

'I told you—'

'I know what you said,' said Sara quickly, 'but you have to admit Mrs Proctor doesn't behave like a—a casual acquaintance.'

Matt groaned. 'What does it matter to you?'

Sara stared at him. 'It matters,' she said huskily, and then, shaking her head, she started towards the door. 'I—I'll see what Rosie's doing.'

'Don't!'

His hoarse command resonated through every nerve in her body, but before she could do anything more than register the fact that Matt was as aroused by their exchange as she was they heard the sound of Rosie's footsteps scampering along the hall towards them.

At once, Matt turned back to the window, adjusting the fit of his shorts with an unsteady hand. By the time Rosie appeared in the doorway he had control of himself again, but Sara couldn't forget the smouldering look he had cast in her direction in the seconds before Rosie burst into the room.

'Daddy, Daddy!'

Rosie's excitement was palpable and, however he was really feeling, Matt managed a tolerant smile for his daughter. 'Hey, sweetheart,' he said, 'what on earth's going on? What did Mrs Webb say?'

Rosie shook her head, her sooty bob bouncing about her face. 'Mrs Webb didn't say anything,' she exclaimed, wrapping her arms about his waist. 'Uncle Rob is here. He came in a taxi. Didn't you hear it?'

'Rob?' Matt was clearly shocked. 'Rob's here?'

'That's what the lady said,' remarked a drawling voice behind them, and Sara swung round to find a tall fair-haired man standing in the doorway. 'Hey, Matt! Long time, no see.'

Sara saw Matt register the complications that the other man's arrival might represent before he could control his features. Already the man's eyes were turning in her direction, and there was speculation as well as admiration in his gaze.

'And you must be the temporary nanny,' he declared lightly. 'I should have known Seton would fall on his feet.'

'That's Sara,' said Rosie at once, letting go of her father to skip across the room to take her hand. But Matt had recovered now, and his harsh voice overrode the little girl's introduction.

'What are you doing here, Rob?' he asked with obvious exasperation. 'I said I'd be in touch.'

'And you know what they said about the mountain and Mohammed?' Rob was sardonic. 'I thought you might be pleased to see me.' He held up the leather attaché case in his hand. 'I come bearing gifts.'

'I don't care what the hell you come bearing,' retorted Matt flatly. 'You should have let me know you were coming.'

'Yeah.' Rob pulled a face. 'Well, I can see you're pretty tied up at the moment.' He looked at Sara again. 'Nice to meet you, Sara. Nannies are getting better-looking all the time. I'm Rob Marco, by the way. Matt's agent, in case he hasn't mentioned me. I must say, you must have some patience to deal with this bad-tempered bast—guy!'

'Oh—' Sara exchanged an awkward look with Matt. 'We get along,' she said. Then, nervously, 'If you'll excuse me—'

'Me and Sara are going for a walk,' declared Rosie, who hadn't forgotten anything. 'You don't mind, Daddy, do you? Not now you've got Uncle Rob to talk to.'

Sara thought there was a lot Matt would have liked to say but his daughter had effectively silenced him. Instead, it was left to Rob Marco to remark drily, 'Shouldn't that be *Sara and I*, Rosie?' He gave Sara a mocking grin. 'Aren't *nannies* supposed to notice stuff like that?'

'Cut it out, Rob.' Matt spoke before Sara could attempt to defend herself. Then, to his daughter, 'You can go for a walk. But only as far as the cliff path, okay?'

Rosie pursed her lips. 'But, Daddy—'

'Take it or leave it.'

Matt was unyielding, but Sara's attention was suddenly riveted by the speculative expression on Rob Marco's face. 'Hey,' he exclaimed, staring at her, 'I know you.' His brows drew together consideringly. 'You're Victoria Bradbury, aren't you? Max Bradbury's wife. I'd recognise those classy features anywhere.'

Sara's face drained of colour. 'No, I—'

'Sure you are.' Rob was adamant. 'Hell, I saw your picture in the paper just a few days ago.' He snorted. 'Your husband was insisting you'd been kidnapped. I might have known the guy was just covering his backside.'

'Please—'

Sara didn't realise she was begging him not to go on, but it did no good.

'Of course, that wasn't the end of it. Not this time,' Rob continued, apparently indifferent to the dismay on her face. 'Bradbury had apparently had a fall and banged his head, and a couple of days later he claimed it was all a mistake. He said he'd now had a letter from you and that you were staying with a schoolfriend. He reckoned he'd forgotten all about it, but it got people talking, I can tell you. I mean, after what happened to his first wife, it would have been quite a coincidence if you'd disappeared, too.'

Sara's lips parted. 'Max's first wife drowned,' she said, hardly realising she was confirming his suspicions by admitting as much, and Rob pulled a wry face.

'Well, that's the story, anyway,' he agreed drily. 'But there have always been doubts that that was the truth.' Then, as if belatedly acknowledging the upheaval he was causing, he added, 'Well, no worries. I can see you're okay. But—' his eyes switched to Matt '—don't tell me you're the old school-friend, pal, 'cos I won't believe it.'

CHAPTER ELEVEN

MOONLIGHT streamed into the bedroom. Sara hadn't drawn her curtains deliberately. She'd left the window ajar, too, so that she could hear the ceaseless boom of the sea. It might be the last time she could indulge herself in this way, and, although she was tired, she was too unsettled to sleep.

Rob Marco's presence weighed heavily on her mind. Matt's agent was going back to London the next day, and although she had no doubt that Matt would impress on him the need to keep her whereabouts a secret she didn't altogether trust him. She guessed he resented her just as much as she resented his intrusion into their lives. As far as he was concerned she was the reason Matt hadn't finished his new manuscript, and was it that unreasonable to wonder if he might not drop a hint in certain circles, enabling Max to find her?

He had the right connections, after all. He'd admitted that he and Max's brother belonged to the same club, and it would be so easy for him to mention to Hugo that she was staying with a client of his. She could hardly blame him. Matt's sales provided a large part of his income and, if what he'd been saying at supper was true, there was a rather impressive contract in the offing, only awaiting Matt's signature.

So what was she thinking? That she'd have to go back to London, too? The very idea terrified her, but she knew that the longer she put it off, the harder it was going to be.

The news that Max had made her letter public was daunting. She wondered if that had been Hugo's idea. It simply wasn't like her husband to admit that he'd made a mistake. Of course, it was possible that he was still suffering concussion from the fall, and perhaps if she could get back before Max had totally recovered from his injuries he might be persuaded that she'd meant no harm.

Yeah, right.

A shudder racked her slim body, and even though it wasn't a cold night she pulled the sheet more closely about her. Since she had no nightwear, she was obliged to sleep in the nude, and tonight, for the first time since she'd come here, she felt exposed and vulnerable.

Dear Lord, Max was going to be so angry with her. He'd been angry in the past, frequently, but he'd never had such an excuse for punishing her before. She should never have run away as she had; she should have stayed and faced the consequences. The excuse she'd given Matt for her flight seemed such a pitiable thing now that she knew Max was alive and well. Who would believe her story? Her mother? Unlikely. Max? No chance.

Besides, it had been an unforgivable thing to do and she knew it. What kind of a woman was she that she should leave her husband's unconscious body lying unattended at the foot of the stairs? What kind of wife didn't care if her husband was alive or dead?

An abused one, she answered herself bitterly. Only an abused woman would have run as she had. Only an abused wife would have believed that her word would mean less than nothing to the people who mattered. Only someone who was used to being tortured for the mildest transgression would have expected to be punished for a simple accident.

And she hadn't left him completely alone. She'd called the emergency services and left the apartment unlocked so that they could get in and attend to him.

Yet, with hindsight, she realised that that was just another rod for Max to beat her with. He was a wealthy man. A connoisseur of beautiful things. The apartment was full of porcelain and artwork that was totally irreplaceable. He'd accuse her of caring so little for his possessions that she'd been prepared to invite a thief into their home.

Sara expelled a long shuddering sigh. It seemed that everything she'd done since Max's accident had been designed to condemn her. She wondered now what he'd told her mother. If past experience was anything to go by he'd have aroused her sympathy for the mistake he was supposed to have made, at the same time leaving her with the distinct impression that Sara was to blame. Perhaps he'd also implied that she'd left without giving him any warning—which was true!—and in his confused state, he'd naturally jumped to the wrong conclusion.

Oh, yes, she was sure Max's story would exonerate him. And, because her mother thought the sun shone out of his eyes, she'd have swallowed it hook, line and sinker.

Sara sniffed, feeling the hot tears behind her eyes. She despised people who felt sorry for themselves, but right now she couldn't help it. Her mother had always taken Max's side against her, had never been willing to listen to any complaint her daughter attempted to make. Right now, Sara knew, it would be incredibly easy to convince herself that without her mother's encouragement she would never have married Max in the first place, even if that wasn't entirely fair.

Nevertheless, it was true that since her father's death some fifteen years ago her mother had depended on her daughter more and more. The fact that Mr Fielding had died in the course of his work as a police constable had caused her mother both bitterness and grief. She'd been sorry he was dead, but she'd resented the fact that he'd left her with only his police pension to live on. Sara could do nothing to change her mother's belief that she'd been badly let down.

She could never remember her mother speaking of her father without that thread of bitterness running through her words. And although another woman might have gone out and made an alternative life for herself, Mrs Fielding had chosen to stay at home feeling sorry for herself.

Sara had worked to support herself through college. She'd gained admission to a local university, which had enabled her to continue to live at home. She'd done her best to make life comfortable for her mother. But it had never been enough. She had never done enough. Until Max Bradbury came on the scene.

Sara still didn't know why he'd taken such a fancy to her. She was totally unaware that her pale oval features possessed a subtle beauty that Max had insisted was only evident to the discerning eye. She had been flattered by his attentions; she admitted it. And the idea that her mother would never have to worry about money again had been appealing.

Oh, she'd been attracted by his money, too, she conceded wearily. In the weeks before their marriage she'd only had to mention that she needed something and it had been hers. Gifts of cosmetics and lingerie had arrived daily, and she'd learned not to confide her wishes to him. It wasn't that she hadn't appreciated what he was doing for her. It was just that she hadn't liked the feelings of obligation she'd started to have.

Her mother had been in seventh heaven, of course. Max owned property in Bloomsbury, and he'd suggested that Mrs Fielding might prefer to live in a comfortable apartment, free of rent, after they were married, instead of staying on alone in the small townhouse she and Sara had shared.

Max had known what he was doing, Sara thought now. With Mrs Fielding ensconced in her new home there'd been no way she could back out. Besides, she hadn't wanted to. She'd convinced herself she was a very lucky woman, indeed.

Max was older, of course, and he'd told her his first wife had died in tragic circumstances. But that had only aroused her sympathy. She'd believed him when he'd said he'd never expected to fall in love again.

It hadn't been until after the wedding was over that she'd come to realise that Max's interest in her had been inspired by other, less flattering motives. He had seen her as a woman without any protection. A possession he could use in any way he chose.

From the very beginning he'd known she was at his mercy. Even when he'd told her he was sorry for hurting her he hadn't meant it. He'd enjoyed brutalising her too much to abandon his cruelty. There had seemed no way she could escape the hell her life had become.

She shivered now, in spite of the warm summer air drifting in through the open window. Not for the first time she wondered if Max's first wife's death had been the accident he claimed. Perhaps the poor woman had killed herself. If he had hurt her, too, why not?

She so much didn't want to go back to London. But God

help her, what else could she do? She was Max's wife; Max's possession. And he was never going to let her go.

Realising she wouldn't sleep in her present state of mind, Sara pushed back the covers and got out of bed. Not bothering with underwear, she pulled on one of her tee shirts and Matt's old sweat pants. The fleecy lining of the pants was warm against her bare legs and she was comforted by the knowledge that they belonged to Matt, that they'd clung to his long legs as they were clinging to hers.

Then, opening her bedroom door, she went out onto the landing. The house appeared to be in darkness. Mrs Webb was long gone and Rosie would be fast asleep, clutching the furry bunny that always shared her bed.

Sara's lips twitched at the thought of the little girl. She would have so much liked a little girl like Rosie herself. But even if Max had wanted a child she would have done her best to avoid giving him that hold over her. It was bad enough knowing that her mother was at his mercy. She would never have forgiven herself if she'd caused a child to suffer because of her.

She was barefoot and her feet made no sound on the stairs. She didn't know which room Rob Marco was occupying, but she guessed he would be fast asleep, too. He'd delivered his small bombshell and she doubted he had any feelings of remorse to keep him awake.

She was crossing the hall to the library when she became aware that someone was standing in the passageway that led to the kitchen. Her heart leapt into her throat and she was half afraid that Rob Marco had had the same problem as herself. But then Matt said roughly, 'What the hell are you doing?' and the breath gushed out of her lungs in a rush.

'I—I can't sleep,' she replied in a strained voice. 'I came to get something to read.' Then, more defensively, 'What are you doing?'

Matt's shoulders lifted. He was just a shadow in the darkness, but, as if wanting to reassure her, he moved into the shaft of moonlight that speared through the fan-shaped window above the door.

'Would you believe getting a drink?' he asked, pushing his

hands into the pockets of the black jeans he'd worn at supper. His action drew her attention to the fact that the jeans weren't fastened. They looked as if, like hers, they'd been pulled on for decency's sake and little else. He wasn't wearing a shirt either, and his chest gleamed like copper in the pale light.

Sara made a helpless little sound. 'Isn't it the truth?' she asked, and heard his sudden intake of breath.

'No.'

She frowned. 'Are you worried about finishing your book?'

'Oh, yeah.' Matt was sardonic. 'I'm always worrying about stuff like that.'

'You are?' She stared at him and he scowled.

'No, dammit,' he muttered. Then, with a speculative glance up the stairs, he walked past her and opened his study door. 'Let's go in here. I prefer not to risk having my conversations overheard.'

Sara followed his gaze. 'But who—?'

'Walls have ears,' he remarked drily, switching on the lamp beside his desk and holding open the door. 'Are you coming in?'

Sara knew she ought to say no. She insisted to herself that had she known she was going to run into Matt she'd never have come down here. Borrowing a book was such a pathetic excuse, after all. Hadn't she really been hoping to find the decanter of Scotch that was kept on the table just inside the library door? She wasn't in the habit of using alcohol as a sedative, but she had wondered if it might improve her chances of getting to sleep.

Now, faced with temptation, she crumbled. This might be the last opportunity she'd have to be alone with Matt, when all was said and done. With a nervous twitch of her braid, she didn't hesitate before following him into the room.

She'd never been in Matt's study before, not with the door closed and the glow of lamplight to add to the illusion of enchantment. The only other occasion she'd ventured into his domain had been when she'd come to ask him if he wanted lunch, and she remembered only too well how that had turned out.

And he'd been fully dressed then, she reminded herself

tensely, turning her head away from the intimacy he represented. With his hair rumpled and the shadow of stubble on his jawline he made her think of all the things she'd forfeited when she'd married Max. And she was suddenly acutely aware of the seam of the sweat pants abrading the sensitive place between her legs.

To distract herself, she looked about the room, noticing the sophisticated computer on his desk, the laser printer and the stacks of printed sheets, the modem that enabled him to send his finished manuscript over the phone lines. There was a leather office chair behind his desk and a matching easy chair in the corner, and shelves of reference videos and CDs to play on the comprehensive digital system that occupied a space beneath the window.

It was a working environment, yet it possessed a warmth and charm that Sara hadn't noticed on her first visit. Perhaps it had something to do with the huge potted fern that filled another corner, or the many pictures on the walls that reflected his love of this part of the country. Castles and the wilderness of Coquetdale, ruined peel towers and rugged coasts, the impressive bulk of Holy Island, with the magnificent arches of Lindisfarne Priory still standing after years of Viking attacks.

'Isn't that where St Cuthbert is supposed to have translated the gospels?' she asked in a tight voice, desperate for something to say. She was instinctively aware that Matt was watching her and she sensed him shake his head.

'That's Lindisfarne Castle,' he said tolerantly. 'Nothing remains of the old monastery. But it's said that they used the stones from its ruins to build the castle.'

Sara managed a fleeting glance in his direction. 'How interesting.'

'Yes, isn't it,' he agreed without conviction. 'Is there anything else you want to know?'

Sara's shoulders sagged. It was obvious he knew exactly what she was doing; why she was finding it so hard to behave naturally. But what was she supposed to say, for heaven's sake? She could hardly come right out and tell him how she was feeling. He wouldn't want to know that.

'Are there ghosts?' she enquired at last, and Matt's nostrils flared.

'Where?' he countered. 'On Holy Island? Or in this room?'

Sara had to look at him then. 'I don't know what you mean.'

'Yes, you do.' He wasn't having that. 'Personally, I don't give a damn about ghosts, dead or alive. And I don't believe you came down here just to indulge in a discussion about the supernatural.' He impaled her with his dark gaze. 'Did you?'

Sara was defensive. 'You know why I came—'

'To get a book,' interrupted Matt. 'Yeah, you said. I just don't happen to believe it, that's all.'

Sara held up her head. 'Well, you're flattering yourself if you think that I hoped I'd run into you,' she retorted indignantly, and Matt sagged back against his desk and folded his arms across his broad chest.

'Did I say I thought you'd hoped you'd run into me?' he enquired, regarding her steadily. 'Could be you were planning to run away again.'

Sara caught her breath. 'In my bare feet?' she exclaimed. 'I don't think so.'

Matt surveyed her bare toes with a critical eye and Sara had to resist the urge to curl them into the carpet. 'Okay,' he conceded, acknowledging her point. 'So what are you doing, wandering about my house in the dead of night?'

Sara sighed. 'I couldn't sleep.'

'Yeah, you said that.'

'Well—' She gave a nervous little shrug of her shoulders. 'I thought I might get myself a—a nightcap.'

Matt's brows ascended. 'A nightcap? As in cocoa, Ovaltine, or what?'

'As in whisky,' admitted Sara reluctantly. 'I noticed you have a decanter of Scotch in—in the library.'

'Whisky?' His tone was deliberately mocking now. 'You were thinking of using whisky as a sedative? Why, Sara, have I corrupted you?'

Sara looked annoyed. 'There's no need to be sarcastic,' she said shortly. 'There's a great deal of difference between taking a drop at bedtime and swigging alcohol in the middle of the day!'

Matt gave a snort. 'I was not swigging alcohol,' he exclaimed. 'Hey, I was stressed, okay?' He gave her a dark look. 'And, before you jump down my throat again, I'm not blaming you. This is my problem. I'll get over it.'

Sara felt ashamed. 'Is—is the book going badly?' she ventured, desperate to avoid the growing intimacy between them, and Matt gave a dismissive shrug.

'What's that expression? It's going as well as can be expected?' Then, tucking his hands beneath his arms, he gave her a cynical smile before commenting, 'Well, isn't this cosy? I haven't been to a pyjama party since I was in short trousers.'

Sara hunched her shoulders. 'I'm not wearing pyjamas.'

'Don't remind me.' His eyes were narrowed and intent. 'You're wearing my old sweat pants, which is a lot less easy to deal with.' His gaze lowered to the tied waistline. 'Humour me. Are you wearing anything underneath?'

Sara was taken aback. 'Are you?' she countered before she could prevent herself, gesturing towards his jeans, and Matt uttered a colourful oath.

'Don't ask,' he advised her harshly. 'Not unless you want to find out.'

Sara's throat was dry. 'Perhaps I do,' she ventured, staring at him, and Matt closed his eyes to avoid her disturbing gaze.

'Sara,' he said heavily. 'This is—not wise.'

Sara sighed. 'I know,' she agreed huskily. 'But—I'm leaving tomorrow.'

Matt's looked stunned. 'You don't mean that.'

'I do.' Sara swallowed. 'You knew I'd have to leave sooner or later. Now that—now that Rob knows I'm here, I think it's the wisest thing to do.'

'No!' Matt's denial was heartfelt. 'For God's sake, Sara, you know how I feel about you going back to that bastard!' He straightened from the desk. 'Dammit, I don't want you to go.'

Sara stepped backward. It wasn't that she was afraid of him. Afraid of herself, perhaps. Afraid of what she'd do if he touched her.

'Matt—'

'No, don't say anything,' he implored her unsteadily. 'I don't want to hear you tell me again that you're his wife—'

'I am.'

'But he doesn't love you!' exclaimed Matt angrily, coming towards her, and this time when she retreated from him she felt the panels of the door at her back. 'He wouldn't treat you as he does if he cared about you. You're kidding yourself if you think he's ever going to change.'

Her breathing suspended. What was she doing? she asked herself wildly. Why didn't she get out of there while she still could? However Matt felt about her, there was no doubt that she was the one who'd provoked him, and, while the knowledge excited her, it wasn't something to be proud of.

There was a hunger in the way he looked at her, a deep primitive hunger that shredded her nerves and melted her flesh. She wanted him, she thought incredulously. She really wanted him. She wanted to know what it was like to be loved by a man whose prime objective wasn't to subjugate her to his needs.

She longed to feel Matt's arms about her, Matt's body pressed in intimate association with her own. She longed for him to kiss her; to show his need for her; to validate her feelings with his mouth.

But all Matt did was place one hand on either side of her head and stand looking down at her with guarded eyes. Although she ached for him to touch her, he seemed quite content to look and not touch. His skin seemed very dark in the shadowy light behind him, the glow of the lamplight creating an aura of brightness around his powerful frame.

There was a faint covering of dark hair on his chest that arrowed down to his navel. A film of perspiration at his nape caused his hair to cling to the side of his neck. She wanted to touch him so badly she was trembling. Did he have any idea what his prolonged scrutiny was doing to her?

'Do you love him?' he asked at last, when Sara was beginning to feel faint from the power of her emotions.

'M—Max?' she stammered, and Matt's jaw compressed.

'Do you?' he demanded, and her mouth quivered.

'You must know I don't,' she said unsteadily. 'I sometimes wonder if I ever did.'

'So you married him for his money, right?' Matt was matter-of-fact. 'And now you wish you hadn't.'

Sara was hurt. 'Is that what you think? My God, you don't have a very high opinion of me.'

Matt's eyes bored into hers. She had the feeling he could see into her very soul, and it wasn't a pleasant feeling. What was he thinking? she wondered. What kind of a woman did he think she was?

Then, just when she was sure he was going to push himself off the door and move away from her, he lifted his hand and cupped her throat. His thumb probed the curve of her jawline before rubbing roughly across her bottom lip. A plaintive sigh escaped her at the intimacy he was evoking. She felt herself leaning towards him and forced herself to draw back.

'I think you're a very brave woman,' he told her, surprisingly, his hand moving down her throat and over the quivering rise and fall of her chest. 'But you're also a very foolish one,' he added roughly. He paused. 'And that makes me angry.'

Sara took a breath. 'You don't understand—'

'I don't want to understand,' he told her harshly, lowering his head and brushing his mouth against the soft curve of her neck. He parted his teeth and bit her in the hollow of her shoulder, very gently. 'Or I might feel some compunction about doing this.'

Sara lifted her shoulder helplessly to his mouth. But Matt was still supporting himself on his hands. And, although his mouth was doing devastating things to her emotional stability, he was deliberately keeping a safe distance between them.

'Matt—'

'Don't tell me no,' he groaned, his mouth trailing hotly up her throat to her cheek. The heat of his breathing moistened her skin, mesmerising her. And when his mouth slanted over hers she closed her eyes in sensual delight.

'I wouldn't stop you,' she managed breathlessly against his lips, and his tongue slid possessively into her mouth.

Her limbs went weak with longing. Her heart was beating so

loudly in her ears that she couldn't think straight. She wanted nothing more than to sink down onto the floor and let Matt do whatever he wanted with her. For the first time in her life she was totally at the mercy of her emotions. The idea of getting naked with him was just the start.

She put out a trembling hand. 'May I touch you?' she whispered, and he sucked in his breath.

'Can I stop you?' he countered hoarsely, revealing his own weakness. And with a shiver of anticipation she allowed her fingers to stroke over the soft hair on his chest.

He shuddered beneath her caress. When her hand strayed lower, over the flat planes of his stomach to the open waistband of his jeans, he jerked uncontrollably. The hair coarsened as it disappeared below the vee and, unable to stop herself, Sara slipped her hand inside his zip.

He wasn't wearing anything else, she discovered breathlessly. But he was hot and aroused, and when her fingers closed about him he uttered a low moan. 'God, Sara,' he muttered, his voice thick with emotion. And, as if he could no longer support himself, his arms gave way.

His weight crushed her against the door. But she loved it. It was what she wanted, and there was a palpable delight in feeling his erection pressing into her mound. She desperately wanted to push down her pants and his, let the silken length of his hot flesh sink into hers. She was certainly ready for him. In the pit of her stomach a pulse was beating, and she could feel her own arousal pooling between her thighs.

His hands sought her buttocks, finding her soft cleft and hauling her against him. All sanity was suspended. The rights and wrongs of what she was doing didn't apply.

Lifting her arms, she wound them round his neck. Her fingers slid into his hair, scraped possessively across his scalp. Her mouth opened wide beneath the hungry penetration of his invasion. She shared his tongue's sensual dance, returning his kiss with all the heat and urgency of her generous nature.

It wasn't enough. Even when his hand pushed her shirt out of the way and he caressed the swollen fullness of her breasts she wanted more. Then he took one throbbing nipple between his teeth and suckled eagerly, and she knew what she had to do.

Dragging a hand from his shoulder, she fumbled at the waist-band of the baggy pants. She felt a quiver of satisfaction when they slipped obediently down to her ankles. She kicked them off, going up on her tiptoes to try and assuage the ache between her legs. She rubbed herself against him, loving the intimacy it evoked, and Matt knew immediately what she'd done.

'Sara,' he said thickly, and she shivered pleasurably when his hand found its way between her legs and found the throbbing nub within its folds of flesh. 'God, Sara, you are beautiful.' His breath shivered from his lungs. 'I want—'

He broke off then, and without saying another word he pushed himself away from her. Her moan of protest had barely left her lips before he took her hand and pulled her across the room.

She had no idea what he was going to do. But she was very much afraid he was going to sit her down and tell her this couldn't go on. That, however much he might desire her physically, he was not prepared to perjure his soul for her sake.

Yet his hand was gripping hers tightly. And when he paused to peel her tee shirt over her head her fears were overtaken by pure excitement. Would he have done that if he was going to send her away? she wondered unsteadily. And why didn't she feel any shame at her nakedness with him?

When he pushed her down into the armchair she gazed up at him uncomprehendingly. The leather was cool against her bottom, but she hardly noticed. Her eyes were wide, enquiring, anxious even now that she might have mistaken his intentions.

But Matt's gaze was dark and passionate, and when he pressed her back against the velvet cushion behind her and knelt between her parted knees, her breath caught helplessly in her throat.

Then his mouth was on hers, his bare chest crushing her swollen breasts. Her nipples pressed, hard and pointed, against his hair-roughened skin. Her fingers sought the front of his trousers, eager to please him as he was pleasing her.

Matt brushed her hands aside, however, and, drawing back,

cradled her breasts in his hands. His thumbs abraded the sensitive nipples, arousing another moan of pleasure from her.

Then, bending his head, he suckled from first one, then the other, causing her to quiver with sheer delight. She shifted restlessly beneath him, striving towards a fulfilment that had always been beyond her. Even now she doubted her capacity to please either of them. Max had always said she was a sexless bitch.

When Matt parted her legs and began depositing soft sensual kisses along her inner thigh, she groaned in protest. She hadn't known she had so many erogenous zones, but it seemed as if everywhere Matt touched her body turned to flame. Her skin felt thin, sensitised. Every nerve leapt eagerly towards his touch.

Then he reached the apex of her legs, but he didn't stop. 'You're wet,' he said, with obvious satisfaction, and when his tongue probed the damp curls that hid her womanhood she caught her breath. She was helpless to stop what was happening and she gasped as she lost all control.

Her climax was shattering. She'd never had such an experience, and when Matt pulled her into his arms she was crying uncontrollably.

'Hey, baby,' he whispered, his hand cradling her head, comforting her. 'It's okay. I'm still here.'

Sara gulped. 'But you—you didn't—'

'Not this time,' he agreed gently. 'This was for you. Only you. Was it good?'

Sara groaned. 'You know it was,' she said, holding his face between her hands and drawing back to look at him. 'But why? Why didn't you—?'

'It's not what you want right now,' he said, getting to his feet and leaving her feeling strangely bereft. 'You'd better get dressed,' he added, picking up her clothes from the floor and dropping them in her lap. 'It will be light soon.'

'Matt!'

But he had turned away and, suddenly intensely aware of her nakedness, Sara hurriedly dressed again. Then, when the cord on the sweat pants was securely tied, she said tightly, 'Am I supposed to thank you, or what?'

'No!' He swung round, his face contorted with an emotion

she couldn't understand. Then, harshly, 'You are still planning on going back to London, aren't you?'

Sara was shocked. 'I—I have to—'

'That's what I thought.' Matt was laconic. And then, almost defiantly, 'I should tell you that it was I who arranged for your letter to be made public. I'd hate you to find out some other way.'

Her brows drew together. 'You?' She was confused.

'Yes, me,' he said flatly. 'I couldn't risk Bradbury keeping it quiet and maybe setting the police to search for you. I got a friend of mine at the *Chronicle* to deliver your letter himself.'

Sara tried to think. She remembered being surprised at Max's generosity, but now she realised that he'd had no choice.

'You were probably right,' she said at last, hardly capable of thinking at all at the moment. 'Well, at least I'm forearmed.'

Matt stared at her. 'You don't have to go back to him,' he stated harshly.

'I do,' she said. 'I'm sorry.'

'Not half as sorry as me,' he told her contemptuously. 'You're a fool, Sara, but not as big a fool as me for getting involved with you.'

CHAPTER TWELVE

IT WAS after eight o'clock in the evening when Matt heard someone at the door.

It was the dogs who warned him first. They'd started barking as soon as the car had turned into the private road that led up to the house, and by the time it pulled into the driveway they were frantic. Matt was torn between the desire to go and quieten them—before they woke Rosie—and seeing who it was.

He had no idea who might be calling at this time of the evening. He didn't get too many visitors at all, and his parents were away in Italy at the moment, enjoying a tour of the wine country.

It could be Emma, of course. Since Sara had left, she'd become almost too friendly for his liking. She seemed to see the other woman's departure as an opportunity for her to prove how helpful she could be, and, despite his protests, she'd insisted on collecting Rosie from school at least three times this week. But he didn't think it was Emma. He'd been distinctly short with her on the phone that afternoon.

His own moods swung from enforced cheerfulness, for Rosie's sake, to total despair when he was on his own. It was a week since Rob Marco had returned to London, taking Sara with him, and nothing seemed to make any sense any more.

The morning she'd left was engraved in his memory. She hadn't come downstairs at all until after he'd taken Rosie to school. When he'd returned she'd been sitting in the kitchen with Rob and the housekeeper, already wearing the voile dress and high heels she'd arrived in.

It was obvious she'd wanted to save his daughter any more distress than necessary. But that hadn't prevented him from feeling sick to his stomach that she'd meant what she'd said when she'd insisted she had to leave.

However, Rob's presence had prevented him from saying

anything stupid. Besides, he'd had the feeling that he'd already burnt his boats as far as she was concerned. She had no idea how he really felt about her leaving. And even thinking about what she might have to deal with when she got back to her husband had torn him apart.

He'd managed to hide his feelings until after the taxi taking her and Rob to Newcastle Airport had departed. Then, shunning even Mrs Webb's company, he'd locked himself in the study and spent the rest of the day in a morass of self-pity.

Despite its attraction, getting drunk had not been an option. Rosie had still had to be picked up from school that afternoon, and he'd had no desire to ask for Emma's help again.

He'd wanted to keep Sara's leaving to himself. But Emma had turned up at the house a couple of days later on some trumped-up mission and he'd had to tell her. Since then he'd had to fend her off with grim determination.

He supposed he was an ungrateful bastard. Emma meant well, goodness knew, and until Sara had come on the scene their relationship had been moving along quite nicely. Now, however, she seemed to think he was ripe for an affair, and he wondered what she'd seen in his and Sara's association to merit that conclusion.

Rosie had taken a good deal of his patience. She'd been terribly upset when she'd discovered that Sara had left without even saying goodbye. She couldn't understand why someone who'd obviously liked staying there had to leave, and Matt had eventually explained that Sara had a husband and family back in London.

The trouble was, Rosie kept asking about Sara's husband. She'd wanted to know if they had any children and why she couldn't write to her from time to time and tell her how she was getting on.

'I'm sure she'd like to know, Daddy,' she'd said, just the day before, and, although Matt was fairly sure that was an accurate assessment, there was no way Sara would be able to justify any communication from them.

It was thinking of her, living with her husband again, that was a constant torment. He'd scoured the newspapers daily, expecting to find some item detailing Sara's return. He'd been sure Max Bradbury would miss no chance to gain a bit of publicity, particularly of a positive nature. And he'd want the world to know that his second wife was safely home again.

Now, however, the dogs' barking was getting the better of him. Deciding that whoever was at the door would have to wait, he strode out of the sitting room and into the kitchen. Opening the back door, he made straight for the dogs' compound. They were instantly reassured by his arrival and, bending, he unlocked the gate and let them out.

He was trying to prevent them from jumping all over him when a man came around the side of the house. He was a large man, with a protruding stomach and an extravagant moustache. Matt wasn't alarmed. He was a big man himself, well able to take care of himself. And, although the other man's appearance was unexpected, he looked more flustered than aggressive.

'Mr Seton?'

'Yes.'

Matt had barely given his response when the dogs saw the visitor. Barking joyfully now, they flung themselves upon the newcomer, almost knocking him off his feet.

The man was attempting to push them off when another man appeared. 'Hugo,' the second man was saying impatiently, 'what the hell is going on?' Then he saw Matt and his eyes narrowed speculatively for a moment before a disarming smile lifted the corners of his full mouth. 'I'm so sorry,' he exclaimed, in an entirely different tone. 'We seem to be causing something of a disturbance.'

Matt faced the two men warily. Even without hearing his brother's name he'd have known Max Bradbury anywhere. Apart from the fact that he'd seen his face on the covers of a dozen magazines and periodicals, the man exhibited a smug self-satisfaction that Matt found both provoking and unpleasant. Visions of Sara's bruised and battered body kept flashing in front of his eyes and he longed to grab Bradbury by the throat and knock that complacent smile off his well-fed face.

It was lucky the dogs chose that moment to transfer their attentions to Max. Barking excitedly, they lunged towards him, and Matt had to grab them by the scruffs of their necks to hold them back. He was tempted to let them do their worst, but that would achieve nothing, Instead, he bundled them back into their pen, and by the time he straightened he had himself in control again.

'Can I help you?'

Max Bradbury came forward, bypassing his brother without even a backward glance. 'Oh, I hope so,' he said warmly, holding out a fleshy hand for Matt to take. 'I do hope so, Mr Seton. It is Mr Seton—the famous *Matt Seton*—isn't it?' he inserted ingratiatingly before going on. 'Allow me to introduce myself: I'm Max Bradbury. And this is my brother, Hugo.' He gave a dismissive little shrug. 'You may have heard the name, but that's not important now. What is important—imperative, in fact—is that I get in touch with my wife. I'm given to understand that Victoria may have been staying with you in the past two weeks.'

Whatever Matt had expected, it wasn't this. Compelled to shake the other man's hand or risk offending him before he knew why he was here, Matt took a second to consider his words. But his mind was buzzing with the apparent news that, as far as Max Bradbury was concerned, Sara was still missing. Had she changed her mind about going back? he wondered, trying to contain his own agitation. Or, dear God, had Bradbury done something to her and coming here was just a ploy to cover his actions.

'Your wife?' Matt echoed at last, surreptitiously wiping Max Bradbury's sweat from his palm. Then, hoping he didn't sound too concerned, 'I'm sorry. I don't know any Victoria Bradbury, I'm afraid.'

Max's eyes briefly flashed with an anger he couldn't conceal and Matt was slightly reassured. Sara's husband wasn't acting like a man in control of the situation. But then Max's smile returned as he continued, 'Perhaps I should have said Sara, Mr Seton. Sara Fielding. Victoria—that is to say, my wife—may be using an alias.' He gave an amazingly convincing chuckle. 'I'm sure you appreciate the advantages of travelling incognito yourself.'

Matt was hardly listening to him. He was wondering how the hell Bradbury had traced his wife here. He had to have been given some clue to turn up on his doorstep. But who was likely to have helped him? Dammit, he needed time to think.

Rob? He frowned. He couldn't believe his agent would have done it. Rob was many things, but he wasn't a grass. He knew what Matt had said about keeping Sara's whereabouts to himself.

He saw Hugo Bradbury watching him over his brother's shoulder and wondered what he was thinking. He was clearly younger than Max and, if Matt wasn't mistaken, he was also rather obviously gay. He looked as if he wasn't happy with the situation either, and Matt guessed he had come here under duress. Sara had said that her brother-in-law was harmless, but Matt reserved judgement. He'd done little to help her when all was said and done.

'I'm afraid I can't help you, Mr Bradbury,' Matt said shortly, eager to get on the phone to Rob and clear him of any involvement. He also wanted to know where Sara had gone after they'd reached Heathrow. He hadn't spoken to his agent since he'd put off signing the new contract. He guessed Rob would still be fuming over what he saw as a deliberate endangerment of Matt's career. But the man wasn't vindictive. 'I'm sorry, Mr Bradbury,' he added. 'There's no Sara Fielding here either.'

Max's smile thinned. 'But she has been here, hasn't she?' he persisted, glancing towards the house as if he suspected Sara might be hiding inside. 'My information was quite specific, Mr Seton. There has been a young woman called Sara staying here, acting as a temporary nanny for your daughter, I believe?'

Matt stifled a curse. 'Well, yes. That's right,' he agreed at last, knowing there was no point in denying something that seemed to be public knowledge. 'But her surname wasn't Fielding, Mr Bradbury. It was something else entirely. In any case, she left a week ago.'

Max's nostrils flared. 'Nevertheless, I would like to speak to her,' he said, his control slipping a little. 'I've travelled a long way, Mr Seton. Surely you can understand my concern.'

Matt was tempted to tell him exactly what he thought of his

so-called concern. That it was his behaviour that had driven Sara to run away. But then he remembered: as far as the public at large was concerned Sara was staying with a schoolfriend. Wasn't Bradbury being rather reckless in risking exposing that story for a lie?

'I'd be interested to know why you thought you might find your wife here,' Matt ventured at last, holding the other man's gaze with innocent speculation. 'Is she missing?'

Max took what Matt realised was a calming breath, and his own anger swelled at the knowledge of how often the man must have used his anger against his wife. He could see the fury in Max's eyes, glistening below the surface of congeniality. Was he wondering how much he needed to say to persuade Matt to tell him what he needed to know?

'I haven't seen my wife for a couple of weeks,' he conceded at last, ignoring his brother's sudden murmur of disapproval. 'She's perfectly all right. I had a letter from her assuring me that all was well. But I'm afraid she didn't tell me where exactly she was staying, and in the circumstances I've been left with no choice but to try and find her.'

Matt's brows drew together. 'In the circumstances?' he prompted. He knew he was pushing his luck, but he needed to know. 'Is there some—emergency?'

Max scowled. 'You could say that,' he said, without giving anything away. 'But it's family business.' He arched an imperious brow. 'You understand?'

Matt didn't understand, but he didn't see how he could pursue this without arousing Bradbury's suspicions any more than they were aroused already.

'I admire your persistence,' he lied. There was nothing about Max Bradbury he admired. 'I can imagine how daunting it must be, combing the whole country for your wife's whereabouts. What made you think she might be in this neck of the woods? Is Northumberland a favourite haunt of hers?'

'We haven't been combing the country,' put in Hugo unexpectedly, and Matt saw Max Bradbury turn to give his brother a killing look.

But then, as if realising that the statement couldn't be left in isolation, he muttered, 'My brother's right. My wife hired a car from a nationwide franchise. It was handed back to an agency in Ellsmoor nearly two weeks ago. Ellsmoor is, as you know, just a short distance from Saviour's Bay.'

Matt blew out a breath. He should have guessed that Bradbury would get around to checking out the car hire firms eventually. All the same, that still didn't explain how he'd found out that Sara had been here. He'd impressed upon the garage in Saviour's Bay, who had returned the car for him, that his name wasn't to be mentioned.

But Bradbury didn't know that.

'You say the car was handed back to an agency in Ellsmoor?' Matt mused, as if considering the situation. 'I do hope whoever handed it in hadn't found it abandoned. The tides around here can be treacherous. I've almost been trapped myself a couple of times.'

Max's mouth thinned. 'I hope you're not implying what I think you're implying, Mr Seton,' he said harshly, and Matt knew he'd caught him on the raw.

'Oh,' he murmured artlessly, 'you mean because your first wife drowned in the Solent? I suppose it must be very worrying for you not knowing where—Sara, is it?—is.'

Max looked murderous. 'If you know where she is, I'd advise you to tell me,' he snapped. 'I can be a good friend, Mr Seton. But a very bad enemy.'

'I hope you're not threatening me, Mr Bradbury.' If Matt hadn't been so concerned about Sara he'd almost have said he was enjoying this. 'As I say, the young lady who was staying here has left, and without leaving a forwarding address. Even if she was who you think she was, I have no idea where she is now.'

Which was nothing but the truth.

Max sucked in his breath. 'But you must know something,' he exclaimed sharply. 'Was this woman driving a car? Where did she come from? How did she get about?'

Matt shrugged his broad shoulders. 'I'm not on the witness stand, Mr Bradbury,' he replied coldly. 'As you prefer to keep your reasons for wanting to find your wife to yourself, surely I can claim the same privilege for my—temporary nanny.'

Max's cheeks were red with rage. Like his brother, he, too, was a large man, but without the gentling effects of Hugo's moustache. In fact, there was something almost bestial about Max's features, contorted as they were now. The man was a monster, Matt thought starkly. Thank God he hadn't had to invite him into his house.

Max, however, seemed to have realised he was not going to get anywhere by being aggressive. Changing tack, he lifted a hand in mock defeat. 'I can see you are a loyal friend, Mr Seton,' he said, glancing round at his brother. 'This young woman, whoever she is, is lucky to have found such a gallant protector in you. I have to say my own wife does not deserve such blind devotion. Her mother is very ill, you see, and Sara has disappeared without even contacting the hospital once to see how the old lady is faring.'

Matt managed not to show his surprise at this news. Surely Sara wouldn't have run away if she'd known her mother was ill.

'I'm sorry,' he said again. And he was. If Sara's mother was ill, he was fairly sure she'd want to know about it. Max would know that too, of course. Matt suspected Max would say anything to get his own way.

'I am sorry, too,' said Sara's husband now, casting another look over his shoulder at Hugo. 'I am very fond of Alicia; that's my wife's mother, you know. She's a widow, and life hasn't always been kind to her. I've done what I can, but...' He lifted his shoulders, bulky beneath the jacket of his dark blue suit. 'I'm not her daughter. What can I say?'

Matt wondered. Max sounded sincere, but, knowing what he did about the man's character, Matt wasn't convinced. He looked at Hugo, trying to gauge his reactions. The younger man's smile was rueful. A silent endorsement of his brother's comments? Or an acknowledgement that he had already said too much?

'I wish I could help you,' Matt said finally, not meaning a word of it. But right now he'd say anything to get rid of them.

Where the hell was Sara? Why hadn't she contacted her mother? If Max was lying, Matt promised himself he'd pay for it.

A few minutes later Matt was back in the study, jerking up the phone. The Bradburys had departed just a couple of minutes ago, and Matt had watched the car until it was out of sight. Max Bradbury had insisted on giving him his card, which listed all his phone numbers, but Matt had already dropped that into his wastebin. There was no way he'd give Sara's husband the time of day, let alone anything else.

Rob answered on the second ring. 'Marco,' he said flatly, and Matt wondered if he was responsible for the lacklustre tone of his voice.

'Rob?' he said quickly. 'It's Matt. Have you got a minute?'

'Well, well.' Rob didn't sound like a man who was expecting good news. 'If it isn't the incredible shrinking career man!'

'Yeah, yeah.' Matt allowed him his moment of sarcasm. 'I know I was a big disappointment to you when you turned up last week. But I've been thinking things over, and if you express-mail the new contract to me I'll sign it.'

Rob gave a stunned cough. 'You will?' Then he was silent for a moment before saying, 'Okay. What do you want? Your signature never comes without strings attached.'

'You wound me.' Matt tried to sound hurt, and failed miserably.

'That's my line.' Rob was laconic. Then, 'Let me guess: this has something to do with the delectable Mrs Bradbury, doesn't it?'

Matt sighed. 'All right. Yes, it does.' He paused. 'She did get on the plane with you, didn't she?'

'And hardly spoke the whole way,' agreed Rob drily. 'That is one close-mouthed lady, Matt. I'm not used to women blanking me for the best part of three hours. You know that.'

'My heart bleeds.' Matt gnawed at his lower lip. 'So what happened when you got to Heathrow?'

Rob hesitated. 'What is this, Matt? An inquisition? Do I take it she hasn't written and thanked you for taking her in. You did take her in, didn't you, pal? That nanny business was just so much hot air.'

Matt expelled a wry breath. 'Just answer the question, Rob. Did you give her a lift into town?'

Rob sighed. 'No way, man. I didn't even get the chance to offer. As soon as we cleared the Arrivals hall she took off running. I didn't see her again. I guess she got a cab into town.'

Matt swore. He'd more or less expected that. 'And you didn't tell anyone who she was or where she'd been?'

'No.' Rob sounded put out. 'I said I wouldn't and I haven't. Why? Have you had a visit from her husband? From what I hear, that sounds like the way he works.'

CHAPTER THIRTEEN

SARA stood at the window of the bed and breakfast where she was staying in Paddington and wondered for the umpteenth time what she was going to do.

It was a week since she'd left Saviour's Bay—since she'd left Matt—and her decision was getting harder to make, not easier.

At first she'd checked into the small lodging house because the idea of going back to Max immediately after what she'd shared with Matt had been too painful to consider. She'd felt no shame. She might have been unfaithful to Max in word and deed, but Matt had made sure that she returned to her husband as unsullied as when she'd left him.

Which was a contradiction in itself, she thought bitterly. But Max couldn't actually accuse her of sleeping with another man. Well, he could accuse her of it, if that was what he believed, but she could answer honestly that she hadn't.

So why did she have such a feeling of loss because Matt hadn't made love to her with his body? Why was she becoming more and more depressed because she knew she might never see Matt again? She'd always known that they had no future. She'd left him in no doubt of what she ultimately intended to do. So why was she regretting it now, when it was over? When it was far too late to have a change of heart?

Of course, where her heart was concerned there'd been no change. Almost from the first moment she'd set eyes on Matt she'd known he was going to mean something in her life. She had no logical explanation. She'd just known he was a man she could trust.

She supposed she wasn't typical of most women in her situation. After years of being abused by one man, how could she instantly have feelings for another? And, if she did have feelings, how did she know they were genuine? She had so little experience to draw on. So much in her life she wanted to forget.

She didn't know why she was so certain she loved him, but she was. It certainly wasn't because Matt had encouraged her to feel that way. On the contrary, most of the time he'd kept a safe distance between them. What affection she'd had had mostly been from Rosie.

Yet, for all that, she'd known he wasn't indifferent to her. The awareness between them, that had begun that first morning, had grown almost without any encouragement from them. It had started even before he'd seen what Max had done to her. And when he'd tended her bruises and touched her with his lips...

Sara trembled. Was she exaggerating what had happened between them? She didn't think so, but it was too late now. Matt had been attracted to her; he had wanted her to leave Max. But that didn't add up to a lasting commitment. He'd been thinking of her, not himself. He'd wanted her to take control of her life.

If she dared.

She frowned now. She knew she'd changed during those days at Seadrift. For the first time in years she'd had the chance to look objectively at her marriage. Without Max's oppressive presence she'd been able to think for herself again. And what she'd discovered had not been a pretty sight.

She saw now that it was Max who had robbed her of her confidence. Slowly but surely he'd convinced her that she was to blame for the punishment he'd subjected her to. And, although she'd been weak to believe him, she'd been living under so much pressure she'd had no strength left to fight his cruelty.

The guilt was his, not hers, she'd realised. Being with Matt had shown her that there was another way. All she'd needed was time to rest, to relax, to find the woman she'd used to be. And being with Matt and Rosie had been the happiest time of her life.

That was the real reason why she hadn't returned to the apartment in Knightsbridge. She'd needed time alone, to think about the future, to decide what she was going to do. Max still frightened her, of course. She couldn't dismiss three years of abuse in only two weeks. But she was prepared to face him again, to show him that the chains he'd bound her with were broken, to make another bid for freedom.

There was still her mother to think about, of course, and she knew a fleeting sense of despair at the knowledge that she'd get no support from her. But surely if she could show her what Max had done, if she could explain to her why she'd run away…

She wasn't hopeful. However determined she'd been in the past, her mother had always been able to get under her defences, to persuade her she was exaggerating Max's behaviour. She really believed her life would have to be in imminent danger for Mrs Fielding to forfeit her comfortable lifestyle. As far as her mother was concerned she was lucky to live in such luxury.

Still, she had to try. This was her last chance, and if she let Max take control of her again she very likely would die—of heartbreak, if nothing else…

St Jude's Hospital was in Euston Road.

If Sara hadn't been so concerned, the incongruity of its title might have amused her. But when she burst through the doors she was already running on adrenalin and little else.

The idea that she'd been hiding out in Paddington while her mother had been fighting for her life just a comparatively short distance away had horrified her. But until she'd gone to her apartment to speak to her she hadn't even known her mother was ill.

It was a neighbour who'd put Sara in the picture.

'Mrs Fielding had a heart attack a few nights ago,' she'd told the stunned young woman sympathetically. 'Didn't you know?'

'I—I've been away,' Sara had answered abstractedly, and the woman's expression had revealed that she'd read the newspapers, too.

'Of course,' she'd said understandingly, but Sara had had the feeling that she'd put her own interpretation on recent events, as everyone else would have done.

'Anyway,' she went on, 'it was lucky your husband was here

when it happened, wasn't it? It was he who called the ambulance, you know.'

That was when Sara's blood had chilled. Max had been visiting her mother? Max never visited her mother. Indeed, Mrs Fielding had often claimed that it was Sara who stopped him from going to see her. But in fact Max himself had nothing but contempt for the older woman. Though it suited him to keep that from her.

He'd always been repulsively flattering whenever Mrs Fielding had visited her daughter, however. He wasn't a fool. He'd known that she was an invaluable—if unwitting—ally in his bid to control his wife. And, despite her fears for her mother's safety, Sara couldn't believe he'd have hurt her now.

Even so, her heart was beating unpleasantly fast as she approached the reception desk. Stammering a little, she explained that she was Alicia Fielding's daughter. She added that she'd been away and had only just discovered that her mother was in the hospital.

'What ward?' asked the woman dispassionately, and Sara realised belatedly that she had no idea.

'She had a heart attack,' she said, by way of an answer. 'I don't know what ward she's in.'

The woman heaved a resigned sigh and turned to the computer screen beside her. 'What name did you say?' she asked, and Sara knew a moment's panic that her mother's name might not appear on the screen.

'Fielding,' she said hastily. 'Alicia Fielding. She—she had a heart attack.'

'So you said.' The receptionist was hardly sympathetic. 'Ah, yes. Here it is.' She paused. 'Ward 32. Intensive Care.'

'Intensive Care!' Sara fairly squeaked the words. 'Where do I find that?'

'Third floor,' said the woman. 'You'll find the lifts along there.' She pointed an indifferent finger along the corridor to her right. 'They'll probably let you in. The ICU don't keep regular visiting hours, for obvious reasons.'

'Thanks.'

Swallowing convulsively, Sara fairly ran along the corridor

the woman had indicated. She was glad now that since returning to London she'd invested her last few pounds in a cheap summer dress and deck shoes. Although she expected her mother to object, she was glad of the flat heels now.

The lifts were huge things, big enough to take the patient trolleys she'd seen in the A and E department as she'd passed. They moved ponderously, too, and she was biting her lip with impatience by the time she reached the third floor.

She found the Intensive Care Unit without difficulty. There were only two departments on this floor. The other appeared to be a recovery ward for patients from the ICU. But the receptionist had said her mother was in the former.

There was a senior nurse on duty, and she looked at Sara curiously when she gave her name. Of course, Sara thought wearily, she'd probably recognised her. And, even if she hadn't, the name would have given her away.

'Mrs Fielding is holding her own,' she said, in answer to Sara's initial enquiry. If she was wondering why Sara hadn't known about her mother's illness until now she was professional enough to keep it to herself. 'She's in there,' she added, pointing towards a glass-framed cubicle. 'You can go in, but please don't excite her. She's had a really tough time.'

Sara hesitated. 'It was a heart attack?' she asked awkwardly, and the nurse nodded.

'But you'll find her face is rather bruised, too, I'm afraid.' She touched Sara's arm. 'It looks much worse than it really is. That's why I'm warning you. According to her son-in-law— But, of course you must know this,' she exclaimed, with some embarrassment, breaking off.

'I don't know anything,' said Sara fiercely, uncaring what Max would think when he found out. 'As I said before, I didn't even know my mother was ill.' She took a breath. 'Please, do go on with what you were saying. What did my husband tell you?'

'Well…' The nurse was clearly reluctant to be the bearer of bad news, but she evidently reasoned that Sara was a close relative and deserved to know the truth. 'According to Mr Bradbury, Mrs Fielding was in the kitchen of her apartment, making a pot of tea, when she collapsed. She hit her face on the sink, I believe. He was most distressed. I tried to tell him that these things happen all the time, but I think he was worried we'd believe he'd done it.'

The nurse gave an embarrassed little chuckle, but Sara wasn't laughing. The explanation Max had given sounded so horribly familiar to her. On one occasion—just once—he'd given her a black eye. And spent the next few days telling everyone she'd walked into a door.

He'd been careful after that. The injuries she'd suffered at his hands had never embarrassed him again. But the idea that he might have attacked her mother was still incredible. Surely even he would never have sunk so low.

Thanking the nurse, Sara hurried towards the cubicle she'd indicated. Pausing outside, she looked in, her heart beating uncomfortably fast in her chest.

Her mother was lying amid an impressive array of tubes and computer screens, an IVF bottle suspended beside the railed hospital bed. She looked older than Sara had ever seen her, and the bruises on her face stood out in stark relief against her pallid skin.

Oh, Mum, she thought achingly, what really happened? As far as she knew, her mother had never had any heart problems in the past. Was it something Max had said that had caused this? Something he had done? Or was she damning the man without a shred of evidence to support her fears?

Taking a deep breath, she pushed against the swing doors and entered the cubicle. The smell of antiseptic was strong, mingling with the usual odours associated with a hospital ward. The room was warm, too, but not unpleasantly so. The hum of the air-conditioning unit was just one of the many systems running in the room.

Her mother's eyes were closed when she entered the cubicle. But as she approached the bed there were definite signs of awareness. The old lady's lids flickered, before lifting warily, as if she wasn't entirely sure she wanted to see who her visitor was.

Then she saw her daughter and her eyes filled with tears. 'Sara?' she said disbelievingly. 'Oh, Sara, is it really you?'

'It's me,' said Sara, sniffing back her own tears and bending to take her mother's limp hand. 'How—how are you, Mum? I'm so sorry I wasn't here when you needed me.'

Mrs Fielding gazed up at her as if she still couldn't quite believe her eyes. 'Where have you been?' she asked, her voice hoarse and unsteady. 'I—I was so afraid—'

Sara's stomach clenched. 'Mum—'

'I thought you must be dead,' went on her mother urgently, gripping Sara's hand. 'You were missing and I had no idea where you were.'

'But Max had a letter—'

'From you? Yes, so he said. But I've never seen any letter, and I had only his word that you'd written it.'

'But it was in the newspaper, too,' said Sara, wishing she'd been able to tell her mother where she was. 'I'm sorry you've been worried. There was no need.'

'But why did you run away?' protested Mrs Fielding. 'What happened that night? I never believed Max's story. Not when he didn't appear to know where you were.'

The old lady was getting agitated, and, bearing in mind what the nurse had said, Sara endeavoured to calm her down. 'We'd had a row,' she said gently. 'One of many, as I've said before. I—Max fell down the stairs, and I thought he was badly injured. I called the emergency services, but I was afraid they'd blame me, and I—well, I ran away. Cowardly, huh?'

'Oh, Sara—'

'Never mind that. I'm here now, and the nurse says you're making good progress,' Sara added soothingly. She forced a smile. 'How do you really feel?'

'Forget about me,' exclaimed her mother dismissively. 'Sara, why didn't you tell me? Why didn't you talk to me? Why couldn't you have shown me what that monster had done to you?'

'Mum, Mum!' Sara didn't know where all this was coming from. 'It doesn't matter now—'

'It does matter.' Her mother was looking up at her with tears streaming down her cheeks. 'Thank God you're here. Thank God you're alive. I've been so—so worried.'

Sara squeezed her hand. 'I'm all right, honestly,' she said, though she was becoming more and more convinced that Max must have played a part in her mother's collapse. 'It's you I'm worried about. Why didn't you tell me you'd been feeling unwell?'

Her mother moved her head from side to side on the pillow. 'Because I hadn't been,' she said simply. 'When you—when you disappeared that evening I was worried, of course. But then Max said you were staying with a schoolfriend, and I suppose I accepted that. He—he had always been so—so kind to me, as you know, and I actually felt sorry for him because he seemed so—so alone.'

Sara nodded, sure she knew what was coming next. She had been the victim of Max's frustrations too many times not to see a pattern here.

'Did—did he do this?' she asked huskily, her free hand brushing her mother's cheek, but Mrs Fielding only grasped both her hands in a surprisingly strong grip and held on.

'Listen to me,' she said fiercely, her eyes glancing towards the door, as if she was half afraid they were going to be interrupted before she could finish what she had to say. 'Sophie Bradbury came to see me, Sara. Sophie Bradbury. What do you think about that?'

Sara blinked. 'Who?'

'Sophie Bradbury,' said her mother again. 'Well, I don't know what she calls herself these days. But that doesn't matter. You know who she is, don't you?'

'Do I?' Sara was taken aback. 'I don't think so.' She frowned, thinking. 'The only Sophie Bradbury I've heard of is Max's first wife. But she's dead.'

'She's not.' Mrs Fielding delivered her news triumphantly. 'She's alive. That's what I'm saying. She came to see me last week.'

Sara's legs gave way, and she grabbed the nearby chair and sank weakly into it. 'Sophie?' She said the name again, as if she couldn't quite believe it. 'Sophie's alive?'

'Very much so.' Her mother nodded vigorously, making the IVF bottle attached to her arm shake alarmingly. 'She lives in the United States these days, but she's been staying with her mother in Bournemouth for the past three weeks.'

Sara was stunned. 'But Max thinks she's dead,' she protested.

'Does he?' The old lady was beginning to look weary now. The excitement of seeing her daughter again was taking its toll, and Sara wondered if she should allow her to go on. 'It may have suited him to believe it. Anyway, when Sophie learned you were missing she was afraid he might have done something terrible to you.'

Sara felt slightly sick. 'Oh, Mum—' She was finding it difficult to take all this in. 'But Max had my letter—'

'Never mind the letter,' said Mrs Fielding weakly. 'What matters is Sophie told me what he was like, what he'd done to her. She was frightened of him, as I'm sure you are. Why, she even had to fake her own death to get away from him.'

Sara could hardly believe it. And now was not the time to remind her mother that she had never believed her before. 'So where is she?' she asked. 'How can we get in touch with her?'

Her mother made a careless gesture. 'I don't know,' she said, and Sara's spirits took a dive.

'You don't know?' she exclaimed. 'Then how do you know she wasn't lying? She could have made the whole thing up. She could be anyone. Some people will do anything to draw attention to themselves.'

'She had photographs.' Mrs Fielding seemed curiously unfazed by her reaction. 'They were of their wedding. Hers and Max's. She got them from her mother to show me, to prove she was telling the truth.'

Sara shook her head. 'I don't know, Mum...'

'Well, I believe her,' replied her mother staunchly. 'I believe she has no reason to lie. I also think she'd be prepared to make a statement confirming Max's cruelty. Particularly now you've turned up safe and well.'

She paused then, looking somewhat anxiously at her daughter. 'You are safe and well, aren't you, my dear? I must say you do look better than you did before you went away. Wha did Max say when he saw you? I'm surprised he let you come and see me on your own.'

'Max doesn't know I'm here,' said Sara flatly. 'It was Mrs Taylor—your neighbour—who told me you'd been ill. She also told me Max was with you when you had your attack. Are you too tired to tell me what he was doing at your apartment?'

The old lady sighed. 'He was hoping I'd heard from you, of course,' she said. Then, 'But that doesn't matter. Let's just say I realise now what a blind fool I've been all these years.'

Sara groaned. 'Max hit you?' she asked, appalled, but Mrs Fielding was shaking her head again.

'No, he didn't go as far as that, but he did threaten me.' She gave a rueful little smile. 'It was when I told him that I knew Sophie was alive that he became quite unpleasant. He accused me of being a parasite, of living on his charity all these years. I'll admit he frightened me a little. But I don't know if I can honestly blame him for my attack.'

Sara was horrified. 'Oh, Mum,' she said helplessly, wishing she'd been there to defend the old lady herself. But then another thought struck her. 'Do you really think he knew Sophie was alive?'

'I think it's possible,' said her mother slowly. 'He didn't seem as shocked as I expected he would be at the news. But I don't think he found out until after he'd married you. The fact that he was already married again must have been a strong deterrent to exposing the truth.'

'Yes.' Sara was still incredulous.

'Sophie is here because she wants a divorce, and after all this time, she knows she can get one fairly easily. It may not be necessary, of course. I'm not sure what happens in these circumstances.'

'Lucky Sophie.' Sara couldn't help feeling envious. She wished Max was out of her life, too. She wished she was free to be with Matt again.

But her mother wasn't finished.

'You know what this means,' she persisted, tiring rapidly now, but determined to finish what she had to say. 'When Max married you he was still married to Sophie. Maybe your marriage isn't legal. You could be a free woman, Sara. And no one would be more relieved about that than me.'

It was early evening when Sara arrived at the apartment in Knightsbridge that she and Max had shared for the past three years.

She hadn't left the hospital until about half an hour ago. Although her mother had been exhausted after her revelations, and had slept for most of the afternoon, Sara had wanted to stay until she woke up again.

The nurse had suggested she should go home and come back again later, when her mother was rested, but Sara had declined. She'd wanted to be there when her mother opened her eyes again. She'd wanted to reassure her that she was there and all was well.

Perhaps part of it was that Sara had wanted to put off returning to the apartment. Despite what her mother had told her, she couldn't believe Max would let her go without a fight. If he threatened her or her mother she would tell him she'd use what she knew against him, she told herself firmly. But Max was an unknown quantity. How far would he go to protect his reputation?

She wondered if Hugo knew about Sophie. She didn't think so. Max's brother might be many things—weak being one of them—but she didn't believe he was a liar. Yet, as far as his brother's character was concerned, he did have a blind spot. Without it, surely he'd have seen what was going on.

There were no lights showing in the apartment, but that didn't mean anything. It was still daylight and Sara glanced at her wrist, realised she didn't have a watch, and shuddered in spite of herself. She couldn't help remembering how her watch had come to be broken. The idea that Max might be reasonable was just too unbelievable to be true.

Perhaps she should wait until tomorrow morning, she thought doubtfully. Although it was still fairly early, night was coming and everything seemed different after dark. But she recognised that for what it was: a pathetic attempt to put off the inevitable. She had to speak to Max; she had to collect her belongings

She had to prove to herself, and him, that she was not going to be bullied any more.

Yeah, right.

The trouble was, she didn't believe it.

Oh, she believed what Sophie had told her mother. But what of it? The idea that Max might allow her to live her own life again seemed just as remote as ever.

It would never happen, she thought dully. He was never going to let her go. Already she could feel the chains of his possession closing about her.

She had to make it happen, she told herself desperately. She'd been afraid of him for far too long. Whatever it took, whatever he did to her, she had to stand up to him. She had to break the chains once and for all.

The doorman looked taken aback when he admitted her. 'Mrs Bradbury,' he said, politely enough, but she knew he was assessing her appearance with a critical eye. She knew she looked pale and harassed, and his attitude didn't help things. The man gave a smirk. 'What a pleasure it is to see you again.'

'Thank you, Patrick.'

Sara determined not to let him intimidate her. This was not the man she had once been friendly with. He was long gone, despatched by Max, she was sure, and this man had taken his place. He was always polite, but Sara had always had the feeling that he was Max's ally. She was certain she could expect no sympathy from him.

Now, tugging on her braid, she asked, 'Is Mr Bradbury in?'

'I believe so, Mrs Bradbury,' Patrick replied, pressing the button to summon the lift for her. 'He'll be delighted to see you, I'm sure.'

'I'm sure.' Sara's voice was tight. She walked into the lift. 'Thanks.'

Patrick drew back as the doors closed, and as if that was the signal for Sara's nerve to give out on her she sank against the panelled wall of the lift in mute panic. Weakness, like a debilitating blanket, enveloped her, and she had to steel herself not to stop the lift and send it down again.

Only the thought of facing the doorman's smug expression

kept her from doing so. She was committed now. Forcing her legs to support her, she straightened, watching the indicator light moving through the floors. Three, four, five, six... At seven, it stopped, and she stepped out onto royal-blue broadloom that was inches thick. She was here. Back in the place she had never wanted to see again.

Max's was the only apartment on this floor and the one above. Sara would have preferred a house, with a garden, but her opinion hadn't been invited. Max had said he preferred the privacy afforded by having no immediate neighbours, and in the beginning she'd assumed it was only a temporary arrangement anyway.

How wrong she'd been.

She was approaching the double panelled doors when they opened. She should have known that Patrick wouldn't have been able to resist warning Max of her arrival. His excuse, had he needed one, would be that he'd known Mr Bradbury was anxious to know she was safe and well. He'd primed her welcoming committee, even if it was a committee of only one.

Panic flared again as Max stepped into the hallway and the concealed lighting that ran along the tops of the walls illuminated his smiling face. She wasn't fooled by his apparent pleasure at seeing her. She knew, as he did, that the doorman would be watching their reunion avidly on the CCTV cameras.

'Victoria,' he exclaimed, as she paused to gather her composure, and before she could guess his intentions he had covered the space between them and was enfolding her in his arms. 'My dear Victoria, you have no idea how glad I am to see you.'

Sara's first reaction was to try and get away from him, but experience had taught her it was wiser not to fight. Even so, she was aware that he was squeezing her far more tightly than was necessary. Crushing her ribs, making it difficult for her to drag any air into her lungs.

'Please...' she got out at last, and, as if he hadn't been aware of her discomfort, Max released her to lay a possessive arm across her shoulders.

'I'm sorry,' he said, his eyes glinting with cold malevolence. 'Was I hurting you? Well—' he urged her towards the door and into the apartment '—put it down to my delight at seeing you again, Victoria.'

As soon as they were through the door Sara struggled free of him, however. Without Patrick's unseen eyes monitoring her every move she felt more prepared to defend herself. She had to defend herself, she told herself grimly. If Max hurt her, this would be the last time he had the chance.

So why did that sound so hollow?

Max closed the doors behind him. The click they made caused a shiver of apprehension to feather her spine but she tried not to show her fear.

Max was looking at her with an expression of satisfaction he didn't try to disguise. 'Victoria,' he said at last, the breath he took expanding the buttonholes on his waistcoat. 'How good of you to grace me with your presence. I must admit, I was beginning to have my doubts about you. But whatever are you wearing? And your hair... My dear, you look like a refugee. Still, I'm happy to see you've come to your senses at last.'

'I haven't—' Sara broke off, licking her dry lips. Then, stepping back into the elegant drawing room behind her, she added, 'I haven't come to my senses, Max. Or at least, I have. That is, I'm not staying. I'm leaving you, Max. I've seen my mother and I know about Sophie. About how she faked her own death to get away from you. You can't stop me—'

'Hey...' Max came away from the door, spreading his hands in a gesture that on anyone else would have looked conciliatory. Following her into the drawing room, he assumed an expression of mild indignation. 'Have I said I'm going to try and stop you, Victoria? Just because your mother's been filling your head with lies doesn't mean we can't sort things out. The woman's senile, for heaven's sake. You must know that. I was half afraid she was going to accuse me of assaulting her!'

'I bet you were.' Sara moved, putting the width of a Regency striped sofa between them. 'You must have got quite a shock when she collapsed.'

'I did. Of course I did.' Max was defensive now. 'I had no idea what the crazy old bat was likely to say next.'

'That you threatened her, perhaps?' suggested Sara, before

she could lose her nerve. 'You didn't like what she was saying so you lost your temper, didn't you? That was a mistake, Max. You've lost your strongest ally.'

Max's broad face hardened. 'I don't need allies,' he said indifferently. 'I have you.'

'You don't.' Sara knew her voice wasn't as strong as she'd have liked, but that couldn't be helped. 'Didn't you hear what I said, Max? I'm leaving you. I—I only came back to tell you goodbye.'

Max sighed. 'My dear Victoria, you know you don't mean that. If you'd really wanted to leave me you'd have sent me another letter.' He paused. 'Where have you been, by the way? I think I deserve an explanation.'

'You don't deserve anything.' Sara quivered with indignation. 'You've been lying to me for years.' She took a breath. 'How long have you known Sophie is still alive?'

Max shrugged. 'Sophie?' He made a careless gesture. 'My first wife is dead, Victoria. She was drowned in the Solent ten years ago.'

'That's not true.' Sara was amazed he would think she'd still believe it. 'She only pretended to drown. With her mother's help she escaped to the States. She's been living there ever since. You know that.'

Max shook his head. 'I know that's what your mother says,' he said patiently, almost as if he was speaking to a child. 'But it's not true. And, even if it was, it has nothing to do with us.'

'It does.' Sara was desperate. 'If Sophie is alive, you were not free to marry me.'

'You're wrong.' He was smug. 'Sophie was legally declared dead before our marriage could take place.'

'Even so—'

'Face it, Victoria. We are married. Do you think I'd make a mistake like that?'

'But our marriage is a mockery,' protested Sara, her hopes for the future fading before her eyes. 'I—I want a divorce.'

'I don't.' Max was infuriatingly casual. 'And if there's the slightest chance that I may have overlooked something, we can easily rectify it. I'll arrange for us to—how shall I put it?—

restate our wedding vows. Yes, that sounds good. No one but ourselves need know why we're doing so.'

'No!' Sara's jaw dropped. 'Do you honestly think I'd do something like that?' she gasped. 'You are crazy.'

'Like a fox,' said Max drily, but his mouth had tightened ominously even so. Then, obviously making an effort to control himself again, he said, 'You still haven't told me where you've been, my dear.' He arched a quizzical brow. 'Or would you like me to tell you?'

Sara was taken aback, and showed it. 'You don't know where I've been,' she said quickly, but Max merely bared his teeth in a mocking smile.

'I'm afraid I do,' he said. 'I know exactly where you've been hiding yourself. And who with. A charming young lady in Ellsmoor heard me asking about you and kindly volunteered the information I needed. I think her name was Proctor. Is that right? Emma Proctor? She was very kind.' Then his features hardened again. 'So, how long have you known Matt Seton?'

Sara's fingers gripped the back of the sofa. She wanted to tell him she didn't know what he was talking about, but she was very much afraid her face had given her away.

'I—I told you in my letter,' she insisted. 'I've been staying with friends—'

'Not *friends*,' Max contradicted her harshly, leaning across the sofa and imprisoning her white-knuckled hands beneath his. 'One friend, Victoria.' His face contorted. 'I repeat, how long have you known Seton? How long has he been your lover?'

'My lover!' Sara could feel all the blood draining out of her fingers as Max's grip tightened. But it wasn't that that caused her breath to strangle in her throat. 'Matt Seton's not my lover!'

'Isn't he?' Max knelt on the sofa to increase his hold on her. He stared at her intently. 'So why are you looking so guilty?'

'I'm not looking guilty.' But she was, and she knew it. 'You're hurting me.'

'I can hurt you a whole lot more than this,' snarled Max savagely. His lips curled. 'Who would have thought it? My frigid little wife has the hots for a famous author. I wonder how

long his sales will hold up when my publicity people are
through with him? Dare you risk that?'

'Oh, I think my public has more sense than to believe an
abusive bastard like you,' remarked a casual voice from the
doorway, and Sara looked beyond Max to see Matt and Hugo
standing watching them. 'And I suggest you let go of Sara. At
once, if you don't mind. We don't want any more visible signs
of your cruelty on her when she files for her divorce.'

CHAPTER FOURTEEN

SARA took the train to Newcastle, spent the night at the Station Hotel, and hired a car to drive north the following morning.

Needless to say, she hadn't slept. Although she was excited at the prospect of seeing Matt again, she couldn't help wondering if she wasn't being too presumptive. After all, Matt was a famous man. He could pick and choose his friends, male as well as female. The very fact that he hadn't been in touch with her since he returned to Northumberland three months ago should have been enough to give her pause.

Maybe she should have waited for him to contact her. He was bound to visit London some time. Or should she have phoned him before recklessly boarding the train? Just because he hadn't wanted her to go back to Max that didn't mean he wanted her himself.

The truth, which was always the hardest to stomach, was that she wanted to see him. She was desperate to see him, actually, she thought ruefully. She had to know if they had a future together. She had to know if his kindness to her had been motivated by pity—or love.

Judging by the weeks and months that had gone by since he'd left London, the former seemed infinitely more probable. She'd known he felt sorry for her, that he'd wanted to protect her. Why couldn't she get her head round the fact that that was all he wanted? Why did a little voice inside her keep insisting that they deserved another chance?

If they'd had the opportunity to talk three months ago things might have been different. Clearer, certainly. As it was, all she had to go on was the stand he'd taken on her behalf when Max had been threatening her; his support when she'd explained that she'd been protecting her mother. And his efforts to ensure that until she got her divorce she had a place to live.

The scene Matt and Hugo had interrupted in Max's drawing

room was indelibly printed on her mind. Despite what had happened since then, subconsciously she kept replaying it in all its awful detail, reliving the moment when Max had realised he had underestimated his enemy.

Underestimated his brother, too, she remembered. It was Hugo who had let Matt into his brother's apartment; Hugo who had told him about Mrs Fielding's heart attack and his fears that Max might have had something to do with it.

To begin with Max had tried to bluff it out. He'd tried to convince Matt that he'd only been teasing his wife by threatening him; that he was jealous.

Of course, he hadn't known how intimately Matt had come to know her, that anything he said would be suspect to a man who'd seen what he'd already done to her in the past. He'd probably hoped that he could deceive Matt as he had deceived her mother. Certainly when he'd released her and got up from the couch there'd been nothing but bland geniality in his face.

Matt, however, had had a different agenda.

'Pack an overnight bag, Sara,' he'd said, ignoring Max's protestations as if he wasn't there. 'You can collect the rest of your clothes later.'

And, because that had been exactly what she'd wanted to do, Sara had obeyed him. She didn't know what had happened after she'd left the room. She'd closed the doors of the drawing room behind her, running up the stairs to the first floor as if the devil himself was at her heels.

It had taken only a few minutes to throw some trousers and shirts into a bag. She'd added underwear, shoes and stockings to the leather tote, sweeping her toothbrush, moisturiser and lipstick into a make-up case.

Then, cramming the bag shut, she'd picked it up and taken a last look around the bedroom she had shared with her husband. Even looking at the bed had caused a sick feeling in her stomach, and, with the bag banging against her legs, she'd hurried down the stairs again, eager to be gone.

She'd half expected to hear angry voices as she'd descended the stairs. She'd been apprehensive of what Max might do if he was cornered. But when she'd opened the drawing room doors again she'd found her husband and Hugo seated together on the couch while Matt had been standing by the window.

Matt had looked relieved when she'd reappeared again. She guessed he'd wondered if she might change her mind about leaving. After all, only days before she'd told him that she had no choice but to return to her husband. Despite Hugo's revelations, he was still unaware that Max's first wife was alive, that her mother's eyes had finally been opened.

Right then, however, it had been Max's face that had drawn her attention. Scarlet with rage, he'd been forced to watch their departure with furious eyes. He'd said nothing, but his eyes had promised retribution, and she was sure it was only Hugo's hand on his sleeve that had stopped him from saying how he felt.

She didn't know what Matt had said to him even now—what he'd done—but clearly it had been enough to prevent any immediate retaliation. Nevertheless, Sara had worried that Max's desire for revenge would overcome Hugo's common sense.

It hadn't happened.

Max himself had suffered a stroke a few days later that had left him severely paralysed and barely able to speak. Hugo had had to abandon the play he'd been appearing in to take charge of his brother's affairs, and he had been more than willing to co-operate with Sara in any way he could.

It had been a difficult time for all of them. And, although Sara hadn't wanted to accept anything from the Bradburys, Hugo had insisted on organising convalescent treatment for her mother when she'd left the hospital. He'd also arranged for the deeds of Mrs Fielding's apartment to be made over to her, ensuring that she would keep her home whatever happened.

He'd wanted to provide an apartment for Sara, too, but, although she'd thanked him, she'd turned him down. Matt had found her somewhere to live until her affairs were settled. A friend of his, another doctor, was planning to spend six months working in the United States and he was quite happy for her to look after his house in Putney while he was away. It had two bedrooms and a garden, and Sara had spent much of the past three months sitting on the patio, trying to make some sense of her life.

Of course, to begin with, she'd spent quite a bit of time at the hospital with her mother. Matt had respected this, but it had meant they'd had little time to talk. Although he'd told her about Max's visit, and his own concern for her whereabouts which had culminated in Rob Marco's supplying him with Max's address, they hadn't discussed personal matters.

She'd been so grateful that he'd run into Hugo outside the apartment building. She doubted he'd have been admitted on his own. And if he hadn't...

But they hadn't talked about that either. Although he'd stayed on for a while she'd known that Matt was eager to get back to his daughter. He'd left her with Mrs Webb and her family while he'd made the trip, but he couldn't stay away indefinitely.

Nevertheless, he had been a tower of strength when Max had had his attack. And when Sara had tried to blame herself for being the cause of it he'd put her straight.

'You have to stop feeling guilty for being a victim,' he'd said, just a couple of days before he'd returned to Northumberland. 'Max had been living on the edge for far too long. His blood pressure must have been sky-high. It was only a matter of time before he snapped.'

Sara suspected he was right, but it had put another obstacle between them. There was no way they could talk about their future with Max lying paralysed in a hospital bed. It was only now, with her initial decree for divorce in her bag, that she felt able to come here and find out if she meant anything to him. Or whether circumstances had blinded her to the obvious: that she was merely another patient to add to his casebook.

She'd read most of Matt's books now. Although his kind of hard-edged crime novel wasn't usually her choice of fiction, she'd found his style of writing fascinating. The main character in all his books was a criminal psychologist, and she'd seen Matt himself in the intelligent caring man he wrote about.

She'd seen, too, that apart from his special treatment of her she had no real reason for believing she was any different from any of the women in his novels. Some of them became attracted to the character he wrote about, but at the end of every book the man was on his own again.

Was that how Matt wanted to live his life? she wondered anxiously, as the signs for Ellsmoor began to appear on her right. Was she only asking for more pain by coming here? Pain of a different sort, and far more devastating?

She had to find out. She couldn't go on not knowing. It was killing her. Living every day as if it was her last.

She passed Rosie's school just as the children were streaming out of the classroom for the morning break. She was tempted to stop and speak to the child, but she knew that was just a delaying tactic. But it did make her think.

Although Rosie had been keen enough for her to be her nanny, Sara didn't know how she'd feel about anything else. Would she want to share her father's affections with another woman? Sara's experience, limited as it was, didn't condition her to expect any happy endings.

It was nearly eleven o'clock when she turned into the private road that led up to Matt's home. Her hands were slippery on the wheel of the hired car, but she succeeded in turning into the gates of Seadrift and drawing the car to a halt in front of the house.

It was amazing how familiar everything looked. It was a warm sunny morning, and the walls of the house were bathed in a mellow light. Her eyes moved beyond the house to the cliffs and the ever-changing sea beyond, and she took a deep breath. She had the most ridiculous feeling that she'd come home.

Although she'd have liked to go round to the back of the house, she rang the front doorbell instead, stepping back a little apprehensively when she heard footsteps in the hall.

Mrs Webb opened the door, her eyes widening in surprise. 'Why Miss Victor,' she began, and then corrected herself. 'I mean, Mrs Bradbury. What are you doing here?'

It was hardly the greeting Sara could have hoped for. 'I— I've come to see Matt,' she said firmly, wishing she felt more confident. 'Could you tell him I'm here?'

Mrs Webb shook her head, and Sara's spirits sank. But the housekeeper only said, 'You've changed your hair, haven't you? It suits you.'

'Thank you.' Sara had had the long hair Max had always coveted cut to a length that barely touched her shoulders. Then, trying to be patient, 'Is Matt in?'

Once again Mrs Webb shook her head. 'I'm afraid he's not,' she said, briefly dashing Sara's spirits for a second time. 'He's taken the dogs out, Mrs Bradbury. I believe he's gone down to the beach. Do you want to come in and wait?'

Sara's head turned towards the cliffs and her stomach fluttered in anticipation. 'I—no,' she said, realising there was no way she could go into the house and sit and wait for Matt to come back. 'I—er—I'll go and meet him.'

'Are you sure?'

The housekeeper looked disappointed, and Sara guessed she'd been hoping to hear what was going on. But it seemed fitting somehow that she should meet Matt on the beach. After all, that was where their relationship had changed so dramatically.

'I expect I'll see you later,' Sara murmured, hoping she wasn't being too presumptuous, and, leaving the woman to gaze consideringly after her, she walked away.

She was glad her shoes had only modest heels as she crossed the grassy stretch to the cliff path. Although it was a beautiful morning, dew had soaked the grass and her heels sank into the soft earth. She was wearing a cream silk blouse, and a brown suede skirt, and the breeze blew the lapels against her cheek.

She paused at the top of the path and looked for Matt. And saw him. He was standing with his back to her, at the edge of the water, throwing spars of driftwood for the dogs to rescue. The two retrievers were charging excitedly into the surf, fetching the wood back to him and waiting with wagging tails for him to repeat the procedure.

Sara's heart leapt into her throat at the sight of him. She hadn't realised until then just how much she'd needed to see him, and her knees shook a little as she started down the path.

She didn't know what alerted him to her presence. It wasn't the dogs. They were too busy playing to pay any attention to someone who was still so far away. But Matt glanced around and saw her, and, leaving the animals, he strode across the sand to meet her.

Sara reached the bottom of the path at the same time he did. They both halted, as if now that they were face to face they had nothing to say to one another. Then, feeling it was incumbent upon her to break the silence, Sara said breathily, 'You're wet!'

Matt glanced down. The legs of his jeans were soaked. 'I know,' he said ruefully, but he didn't sound as if he cared. 'You're not,' he added, after a moment. 'In fact, you're looking great. Life must be agreeing with you.'

Sara didn't know how to answer that. But as she continued to look at him she saw that he had lost weight. Although he still looked good to her, she saw that his cheeks had hollowed, there were pouches beneath his eyes, and his mouth had a distinctly cynical curve.

But she couldn't say that either. Instead, she chose to gesture at her own clothes, saying lightly, 'It must be quite a change for you to see me in something decent at last.' And when that didn't provoke any response she went on, 'Do you like my hair?'

'I liked it before,' said Matt indifferently. Then, as Mrs Webb had done before him, 'What are you doing here, Sara?'

Sara took a deep breath and decided she had to be forthright about this. 'I—thought you might be glad to see me,' she said, lifting her shoulders in an embarrassed gesture. 'Was I wrong?'

Matt swayed back on his heels. He was barefoot, she noticed, the cuffs of his jeans rolled to his knees.

'I'm always pleased to see a friend,' he replied at last, which wasn't at all what she wanted to hear. 'How's your mother?'

'Oh—' Sara was taken aback. 'She's much better, thanks. She's home again now, of course, but a friend of hers is staying with her.' She paused. 'If it works out, it may become a permanent arrangement.' She paused. 'Her friend is a widow, too.'

'Sounds like a good idea,' said Matt evenly. 'And Max?'

'Max?' She swallowed. 'I believe he's making good progress. He's still paralysed. I don't think that will change. But his speech is improving.'

'That's good.'

'Yes.' Sara didn't know what else to say, so she took the easy way out. 'My mother asked me to thank you for what you did. She's very grateful. We both are.'

Matt's nostrils flared for a moment. 'It was my pleasure,' he said politely. Then, carelessly, 'I expect you've been busy. Dave says you've kept him up to speed on the house. Do you think you'll stay there the full six months?'

I hope not, thought Sara anxiously. Dave Sloan was the doctor whose house Sara was living in. But it was another opening. 'Has he been in touch with you? He didn't mention it.'

'Why would he?' Matt's tone was cooler now. 'As far as Dave is concerned we're just acquaintances. He probably assumes you used to be a patient of mine.'

'And was I?' asked Sara, desperate to break through the wall Matt was steadily erecting between them. 'Was that all I was to you? Just another specimen for your casebook?'

'Don't be so bloody stupid!'

Matt turned away from her now, whistling for the dogs that had strayed further along the beach. He seemed as far away from her as ever, and in spite of what he'd said she sensed he wished she'd never come here.

Moving until she could see his face again, she touched his arm and was startled when he pulled away from her. He was wearing a sleeveless tee shirt and his skin was chilled beneath her fingers.

'You're cold,' she said, without thinking, and he looked at her with eyes that were as dark and bruised as hers used to be.

'Look,' he said grimly, 'there was no need for you to come all this way just to thank me for helping you. A phone call would have sufficed.'

'Not for me,' said Sara fiercely. 'I wanted to see you again.' She waited a beat. 'I thought—I hoped you might want to see me, too.'

'I am pleased to see you,' said Matt, but there was no warmth in his voice. 'It's good to know that you've taken control of your life again.'

'Is it?' Sara pressed her lips together. 'Why do I get the

feeling that you don't mean that? What's wrong, Matt? We used to be so—so close. Now—now you're acting like we're strangers.'

'We are strangers, Sara,' he said quellingly. 'I was there when you needed someone. Don't try and make it into something different. It doesn't work.'

Sara stared at him. 'Is that what you think?'

'It's what I know,' he told her flatly. The dogs were racing towards them now, and he moved to deflect their noisy excitement. 'Go find someone else to play with. I'm too old for these games.'

'What games?' Sara was trembling. 'I think you're mixing me up with someone else.'

Matt glanced over his shoulder. 'It's not me who's doing the mixing,' he said coldly. Then, as the dogs reached him and he grabbed for them, 'I just hope you know what you're doing, Sara. Because, God help me, I don't.'

'Obviously not.' Sara gulped. 'You clearly have no idea how much courage it took for me to come here.' Turning, she looked up the cliff path through eyes that were virtually blinded with tears. 'Don't tell me you don't know why I came,' she added in a muffled voice, 'when what you really mean is that you hoped you'd seen the last of me!'

She heard his sudden intake of breath a moment before the dogs reached her. Her words had evidently surprised Matt, perhaps causing him to momentarily relax his hold on the animals. Whatever, Sara was suddenly assaulted by two damp squirming bodies whose wet noses and sandy paws showed no respect at all for her or her clothes.

She gasped, staggering back under their exuberance, helpless laughter mingling with her tears. They were so excited, so welcoming, that she wanted to wrap her arms about them and bury her tear-stained face in their soft fur.

Her heel turning on a pebble gave her her wish. Without anything to save her she lost her balance, and the weight of the dogs bore her back onto the sand.

For a moment she was overwhelmed by doggy breath and

licking tongues, and then Matt was hauling them off her, his anger causing even the retrievers to cower away from him.

'God, I'm sorry,' he apologised, helping her to sit up. 'Crazy beasts!' Then he saw the tears on her face. 'Did they hurt you?'

Sara shook her head. 'No more than you did,' she said unsteadily, but when she would have got to her feet Matt stopped her.

'Don't say things like that,' he muttered. 'How did I hurt you? All I did was give you time to come to terms with what had happened. And you have.'

Sara looked up at him. 'And that means—what?'

An expression of weariness crossed Matt's lean face. 'You know what it means.' His tone was bleak. 'I asked you how Max was and you told me. You've been to see him, haven't you? Several times. You're thinking of going back to him.'

'No!' Sara was horrified that he should even think such a thing. 'I've been to see him, yes. But that was only a—a courtesy. I don't want to live with him again.' She shivered. 'I couldn't.'

Matt's eyes narrowed. 'You don't have to spare my feelings, you know,' he said harshly. 'I know how much he thinks of you; how much he wants you back. And it's not as if he's a danger to you any more. You could call the shots any way you chose to play it.'

Sara stared blankly at him. 'Where is all this coming from?' she demanded. 'Surely you know, better than anyone, that I'd never go back to Max, however sorry I felt for him? I don't hate him any more, that's true, but I don't have any intention of—of staying with him. I've got my first set of divorce papers in my bag if you don't believe me.'

Matt sat back on his heels. 'But Rob said—'

'Yes?' Sara quivered. 'What did Rob say?'

Matt raked an unsteady hand through his hair. 'He said— hell, don't blame Rob. He got it from your husband's brother. Hugo—Hugo told Rob that he's optimistic that you and Max—'

'I don't care what Hugo said. There is no me and Max,' declared Sara, uncaring if her words were ungrammatical. She couldn't take her eyes off Matt. 'Is that what you thought? That Max and I were getting back together?'

'It seemed possible,' said Matt, heaving a sigh. 'After all, you married him. You must have cared for him once.'

'You accused me of marrying him for his money,' retorted Sara, blinking back her tears, and Matt shook his head.

'I know you better than that now,' he told her heavily. 'Dear God, Sara, a man will say anything to protect himself.'

Sara licked a tear from the corner of her mouth. 'Did you need protection?' she asked huskily, and Matt's lips took on a rueful curve.

'You better believe it,' he said, cupping her jaw with one cold hand. His thumb brushed over her lower lip and he bent his head to rescue another tear from her cheek with his tongue. 'I think you'd better tell me again why you came here. I don't want to make any more mistakes.'

Sara shivered again, but this time with anticipation, not from fear. 'You know why I came,' she breathed, and Matt blew softly in her ear.

'Indulge me,' he said, his free hand coming to slide the collar of her silk shirt aside so that he could touch her bare shoulder with his lips. 'My confidence is at a pretty low ebb at the moment.'

Sara turned her face against his rough cheek. 'Didn't you finish your book?' she asked innocently, and he growled his indignation.

'You'll have to get it through your head that there are more important things in my life than my writing,' he told her thickly.

'Rosie. I know.'

'Not just Rosie,' he said, tilting her face up to his. His fingers caressed the skin below her ears. 'Why did you take so long to come to a decision about us?'

'So there is an "us"?' Sara whispered, and once again he made a sound of impatience.

'If you want there to be,' he said at last. 'Do you?'

'Need you ask? And I didn't know if I was doing the right thing by coming here. I've never done anything like this before.' Sara's hands came up to grip his wrists. And when he continued to just look at her she said unsteadily, 'Can't you kiss me? Please! I'm shaking.'

'That's the cold,' said Matt, but something in her expression seemed to wither whatever control he'd been putting on himself. With a groan of submission he linked his hands behind her neck and pulled her towards him and her wishes were fulfilled when his mouth slanted over hers.

Sara groped for him, her fingers encountering the tight fabric of his tee shirt before tearing it free of his pants and burrowing beneath. His skin was warm and masculine, the muscles taut beneath her hands. As her mouth opened wide beneath the hungry penetration of his tongue her breasts peaked against his chest, and between her legs she felt the liquid proof of her arousal.

Oh, God, she loved him, she thought achingly, lying back and drawing him down on top of her. And although Matt protested that she was going to get sand in her hair, too, she didn't care. This was her moment, this was where she wanted to be, and it was just so heavenly to feel his powerful body crushing hers into the sand.

He kissed her many times, kisses that grew more and more passionate, more and more devastating. She felt drugged with emotion, drugged with the sensual urgency of his mouth. And so weak with longing she didn't think she would ever have the strength to get up.

Matt peeled her shirt away from her breasts and she trembled when he said, 'No bra?'

'I didn't think I needed one,' she whispered in answer, shifting uncontrollably when he took one of the sensitive peaks into his mouth.

'You didn't,' he said, rolling the taut areola against his tongue before beginning to suck on it strongly. So strongly that she could feel its pull deep down in the pit of her stomach.

When she felt his hand between her legs, her knees trembled. She shouldn't have worn any pants either, she thought dizzily, as his fingers slid beneath the scrap of silk and lace and found the moist core of her. She arched up against his hand, already aching for a fulfilment only he could give her. But she wanted him, not a replacement, and somehow she managed to push his hand aside.

'Matt—'

But Matt had misunderstood. Bracing himself with his elbows, he lifted himself away from her. 'I know,' he said. 'I'm going too fast. I'm sorry.'

He would have sunk back onto his knees then, but Sara wouldn't let him. With a groan of frustration she grasped the waistband of his jeans, and before he could stop her she'd released the buckle.

'You're not leaving me again,' she said tremulously. 'I want you, Matt. All of you. Not just—not just an imitation.'

'Dammit, Sara—'

He tried to hold the two sides of his pants together, but Sara had already opened his zip, and she stared at him as she slipped her hand inside and caressed him.

'Tell me you don't want me,' she exclaimed, the engorged length of him throbbing in her hand, and Matt was forced to admit defeat.

'Of course I want you,' he admitted, his voice hoarse with emotion. 'Dear God, Sara, I've wanted you since the first time I touched you. You know that.'

'I do now,' she whispered, her fingers going to the button on her skirt. 'Help me, darling. I want there to be no barriers when you make love to me.'

Matt groaned. 'Sara—'

'You're not going to refuse me, are you?' she breathed unsteadily, and he closed his eyes against the unconscious provocation she represented.

'We should go back to the house,' he offered half-heartedly, but she was already easing his jeans over his tight buttocks.

'And have Mrs Webb speculating on what we're doing,' murmured Sara softly. 'I don't think so. Do you?'

'I can't think any more,' admitted Matt, kicking off his jeans without further protest. He tore his tee shirt over his head as she dispensed with her shirt and used it to make a soft bed for them to lie on. 'Here…' He nuzzled her bare shoulder as she attempted to slip out of her skirt and briefs. 'Let me.'

When Sara lay back on the sand Matt went with her, and she was tantalised by the roughness of the hair that surrounded his swollen shaft. She wanted to touch him again, but he wouldn't let her.

'I don't want any substitutes either,' he told her, making her blush. He parted her legs to kneel between her thighs. 'I just want you. The woman I love.'

He entered her in one sleek sure movement. Sara's muscles expanded and then closed tightly around him, so that he moaned a little at the knowledge that this would not last long.

They were hungry for one another, and in a few regrettably short strokes Sara felt her senses spinning away from her. Seconds later Matt joined her, his release pumping hotly inside her. Matt's seed, she thought dreamily. She hoped that one day she would have Matt's baby. A new life to make her life complete...

EPILOGUE

THEY didn't get another chance to be alone together until after Rosie had gone to bed that evening.

The little girl had been delighted to see Sara again. She'd spent most of the time since her father and Sara had collected her from school asking how long she was going to stay, whether she had decided to be Rosie's nanny, after all.

'Sara's going to live with us,' Matt had told her at last, after he and Sara had decided it was the easiest way of breaking the news of their relationship to the little girl. 'She's not going to be your nanny exactly. She's just going to live here.'

'Like a mummy?' Rosie had asked excitedly, and although Matt had been tempted to say *Exactly like a mummy*, he was afraid of jumping the gun.

But Sara hadn't had any such inhibitions. 'Would you mind if I married your father?' she'd enquired softly, and Rosie had hardly hesitated.

'I don't think so.' She'd paused. 'Could I call you Mummy?' she'd added. 'I've never had a mummy, you see. I think I'd like that.'

'You can call me anything you like,' Sara had told her gratefully, giving her a hug. 'We're going to be a real family. Would you like that?'

This time Rosie had had no reservations. 'Yes, please,' she'd said eagerly. 'Will you be getting married soon? Can I be your bridesmaid?'

Sara had looked at Matt then, and he hadn't been able to hide his amusement. 'Why not?' he'd answered blandly, and he and his wife-to-be had exchanged a look of complete understanding over his daughter's head.

Mrs Webb hadn't been at all surprised at the outcome, or so she'd said anyway. 'I always knew you were sweet on her,' she'd said to Matt, causing him to get a little red-faced at the backhanded compliment. 'I'm very happy for you. I'm sure you'll have a great life together.'

But now Mrs Webb had gone home, Rosie was safely asleep in her own bed, and Sara was getting her first real look at Matt's bedroom.

It was a very masculine room, she thought, but it suited him. It suited her, too, she thought languidly some time later, after Matt had made love to her again. The hangings of rust and gold gave the room a warm ambience, and she was anticipating lots of evenings spent here, either listening to music or watching the television that occupied a carved cabinet at the foot of the bed.

Or making love, she reminded herself, with a delicious sense of completeness. Matt had told her he loved her in so many different ways, and it was difficult now to imagine how empty her life would have been if they'd never met.

But perhaps they would have met one day, she reflected. Hugo did know Rob Marco, after all. It was possible that with one of those quirks of fate they might have met, and fallen in love.

But Max would never have let her go, she remembered, the thought causing her to nestle even closer to Matt's drowsing form. And Matt would never have known what Max had done to her if he hadn't rescued her from the sea. She owed him her life as well as her happiness, she thought fancifully. And that was as it should be.

'Are you happy?' Matt asked suddenly, and she realised his eyes had opened and he was studying her grave expression rather thoughtfully. 'You're not regretting anything, are you?'

'As if I would,' she breathed, her lips closing on one of his taut nipples. 'I love you, Matt. I was just thinking how fate plays tricks on all of us. When Max fell down the stairs I thought my life was over. Little did I know it was just beginning.'

Matt rolled over onto his side so that he could look at her. 'I like that analogy,' he said. 'I feel the same. Little did I know when you walked round the corner of the barn that I'd found my destiny.'

'Your destiny?' Sara dimpled. 'That's very poetic.'

'I can write poetry, too,' said Matt drily. 'It's just not fit for public consumption, that's all.'

'I bet it is.' Sara's eyes sparkled. 'You don't do anything by halves. Look at the way you handled Max. I was full of admiration.'

Matt gave her an old-fashioned look. 'Yeah, right.'

'I mean it,' she insisted. 'I've never known Max to back down over anything. What did you say to him? Did you psychoanalyse him or something?'

'Nothing so dramatic.'

'Matt!'

'Oh—well, I guess I reminded him that I had friends in the media, too. And—I also told him that I had pictures of you that would look pretty damning on the front pages of the tabloids.'

Sara gasped. 'But you don't. Have pictures of me, I mean.' She paused. 'Do you?'

Matt pulled a wry face. 'What do you think? That I crept into your room at night and took photographs of your naked body?'

'Well, no, but—'

'He didn't know it wasn't true,' said Matt flatly. 'And once you told me about his first wife I realised why my words must have struck home.'

Sara shook her head. 'Amazing.'

'You don't mind?'

'Mind?' Sara gazed at him incredulously. 'My darling, I was in bondage and you set me free.'

'Now who's the poet?' he asked, his lips caressing her shoulder, and she gurgled with laughter.

'Not me,' she said firmly. 'I'm just a primary school teacher and part-time nanny!'

'And the love of my life,' added Matt, his hand suddenly busy elsewhere. 'Hmm, what was that you said? That I set you free? Well, my darling, do you feel like showing me some gratitude?'

And she did.

Season's Greetings

from

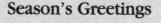

Seduction and Passion Guaranteed!
The world's bestselling romance series.

Treat yourself to a gift this Christmas!

**Enjoy these holiday stories,
written especially for you:**

CHRISTMAS EVE WEDDING
by Penny Jordan #2289

CHRISTMAS AT HIS COMMAND
by Helen Brooks #2292

THE PLAYBOY'S MISTRESS
by Kim Lawrence #2294

All on sale in December

**Pick up a Harlequin Presents® novel
and you will enter a world of
spine-tingling passion and provocative,
tantalizing romance!**

Available wherever Harlequin books are sold.

HARLEQUIN®
Makes any time special®

A visit to Cooper's Corner offers the chance for a new beginning...

COOPER'S CORNER

Coming in December 2002
DANCING IN THE DARK
by Sandra Marton

Check-in: When Wendy Monroe left Cooper's Corner, she was an Olympic hopeful in skiing...and madly in love with Seth Castleman. But an accident on the slopes shattered her dreams, and rather than tell Seth the painful secret behind her injuries, Wendy leaves him.

Checkout: A renowned surgeon staying at Twin Oaks can mend Wendy's leg. But only facing Seth again—and the truth—can mend her broken heart.

HARLEQUIN®
Makes any time special ®

Visit us at www.cooperscorner.com

CC-CNM5

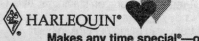